"I came to interview you for my English assignment. It won't take too much of your time," Leah said.

"I'm not in the habit of inviting strangers in," Mrs. Fox replied. "Now be off with you!"

Leah's face fell. "I only wanted to talk to you," she said, her voice trembling. Mrs. Fox *was* a nasty person. No wonder no one liked her.

But when Mrs. Fox saw Leah's crestfallen face, she softened a bit. "I'm busy now," she continued reluctantly, "but you can come back on Monday."

Other Apple Paperbacks
you will enjoy:

My Sister, the Meanie
by Candice F. Ransom

Too Many Murphys
by Colleen O'Shaughnessy McKenna

Ten Kids, No Pets
by Ann M. Martin

Kate's Book
by Mary Francis Shura

A Different Kind of Friend

Vivian Schurfranz

AN
APPLE
PAPERBACK

SCHOLASTIC INC.
New York Toronto London Auckland Sydney

ISBN 0-590-42878-0

12 11 10 9 8 7 6 5 4 3 2 1   0 1 2 3 4 5/9

Printed in the U.S.A.   40

First Scholastic printing, April 1990

For Kay —
a dear and close friend.

1

Leah Dvorak threw down her pen and stared out the window. She hated reading history — hated reading about Jamestown and hated answering these stupid study questions. Watching a squirrel leaping from limb to limb of the huge cottonwood in their backyard, she yearned to be free. But her parents had grounded her for receiving an F on the first history test of the year. She sighed, running her fingers through her thick brown hair. Before they'd lift her grounding, she had to get a passing grade. And she was sure that would be almost impossible.

The sixth grade at John Adams School was much worse than the fifth grade had ever been. Now she had two teachers to deal with instead of one.

Downstairs she heard her mom and dad come in from their day at the coffee shop. Located in downtown Wilmette, Illinois, The Apple Tree

Cafe was quite near Tall Trees Lane, so her parents were usually home by four. They left the house, however, at five-thirty in the morning so they could open for six-thirty breakfast. Then after the lunch hour they closed for the day. Leah and her older brother, Steven, had nice clothes, bikes, and rooms of their own. But sometimes Leah wished they lived in a cabin in the woods where she'd never have to go to school again. Why couldn't she be more like Steven, who got A's in every subject and already knew that he wanted to be an archaeologist? He'd travel to Egypt, Africa, China, and a million exotic places.

A leaden weight grew in the pit of her stomach. Unlike Steven, she had no idea what she wanted to be when she grew up. And here she was eleven years old without even a clue as to what she was good at. If she could only spend her time outdoors.

Reluctantly Leah picked up her pen again and reread the question, *"How was Jamestown governed?"* "Who cares?" she muttered, thumbing back through the chapter and hunting for the answer.

The phone rang, and before she answered, she knew it would be Roseanne Fairbanks, her best friend. Roseanne always called as soon as she got home.

This time, though, Roseanne didn't talk too long because she was off to the mall to meet Danielle Blanchard, Leah's second best friend. "Oh, I wish I could go with you," Leah complained miserably. "I'll be stuck in my room for the rest of the year if I can't bring my grades up. I wish I was smart like you or Danielle." She paused, then asked half-heartedly, "How was cheerleading practice?" She'd wanted to try out, too, but hadn't bothered since cheerleaders had to have a B average. She could just see Roseanne's slender, lithe figure leaping and cartwheeling through the air. Leah was slim, too, and just as agile, but what was the use? Her grades just weren't good enough.

Leah listened to Roseanne tell her that she'd soon be getting better grades and she'd soon be able to join them. But even after the pep talk Leah still felt left out and depressed. "Well," she said, trying to keep her voice light, "have fun at the mall. Remember me slaving away on my history." She gave a short laugh, not feeling funny at all. She hung up, going back to her reading, but the words blurred before her eyes.

"Hey, Leah!" Steven called, knocking on her door.

"It's open," she said.

"Whatcha doing?" her older brother asked. He

sauntered in, hands in his pockets. He was square built and looked more like a wrestler than a would-be archaeologist.

"What else would I be doing?" she answered bitterly, envying how fast Steven finished his schoolwork and still got top grades. It wasn't fair.

"Can I help?" he asked, leaning over her chair and picking up her paper. "You only have two questions finished and ten to go?"

"I hate this junk," she said, trying to explain her slow progress.

Steven flipped back a page. "Here's the paragraph on Jamestown's council," he said, pointing at the middle of the page.

How easy it was for him, she thought. Maybe when you were a high school sophomore you just knew how to study. She appreciated Steven's concern, though. He really wanted her to do better. Then again, maybe he didn't want to be saddled with a dumb sister. Well, that was too bad. He would just have to face facts. She was stupid, and there wasn't a thing anyone could do about that!

Anger suddenly welling up within her, Leah waved her brother away. "All right, all right," she snapped. "I'll do this alone, Steven."

Steven threw up his hands. "OK, OK, just trying to be helpful," he teased.

When he left she stared at the paper and then began to copy the meaningless words. Maybe if she got a decent grade on these study questions her parents would set her free.

On Friday Danielle hobbled into class on crutches, her foot in a cast.

"What happened, Danielle?" Leah asked.

"Baseball practice," Danielle said with a grin on her round face, as she manipulated herself into her desk. She was the star catcher on the Wildcats baseball team. "I shouldn't have slid into first base. Got a broken ankle." Leah jumped up to take the crutches and prop them against the wall.

"Thanks, Leah," Danielle said, handing her a pen and pointing to her gleaming white cast. "Sign," she ordered.

Leah scrawled in big letters:

To one of the Wildcats who got too wild
Leah

Danielle laughed. "Yup! the Wildcats will just have to limp along without me!"

"Look who's doing the limping," Leah countered, laughing with her.

"Danielle!" Roseanne cried, dashing in. "I heard

about your accident! Why didn't you call me? Let's see your cast!"

"Better yet, sign it," Danielle said, her freckled face glowing.

Roseanne bent her blonde head over the cast and intently wrote her name. Roseanne's heart-shaped face had a bright, scrubbed look, and her blue eyes were fringed with long brown lashes. She wore a pale yellow sweater, which brought out golden highlights in her honey-blonde hair.

After Roseanne signed, Danielle pulled a doughnut out of her sack and munched happily. Leah shook her head, smiling. It wasn't even nine o'clock yet, and Danielle was already on her second breakfast. But Danielle stayed in shape playing baseball, volleyball, and soccer.

Danielle licked her fingers, reaching for her pen. "Did you get the answer to number seven?" she asked.

Leah shook her head. "You're asking *me?*"

"Sorry, Leah." Danielle grinned again. "What about you, Roseanne?"

Roseanne took out her neatly done homework, reading off the answer to number seven.

Leah leaned back in her desk. Everything was all right when she was with Roseanne and Danielle. Even if she didn't do so well at school, they liked her, and she belonged. Even if it was only September, and she had nine whole months of school to face, at least her friends were there. That made anything bearable.

A week after her grounding, Leah managed to eke out a C on a history quiz, which meant she could rejoin Roseanne and Danielle after school. What a relief! She was tired of being hounded about her grades. Even Mr. Gonser, her science teacher, had urged her to try harder, saying she could do better. Leah had only nodded, pretending that she'd study more. Well, maybe pretending wasn't exactly the right word. She really *wanted* to study harder, but whenever she settled down to read, her mind switched into automatic pilot and zoomed off into space. She'd rather think about more pleasant things, like horseback riding, or walking in the woods with Roseanne. She hated studying unpleasant things like Jamestown, amoebas, fractions, and Edgar Allan Poe.

In English class Miss Calvert handed out a new assignment sheet for the first major writing project. Carefully, Leah read the directions:

Due October 20th: Interview someone that you'd like to learn more about. Take enough time to really get to know him or her. Try to discover hobbies, likes and dislikes, and what the person's ideas are.

She groaned. Another writing assignment, and she didn't have a clue who she could write about! No doubt about it. School was a bummer.

2

On the way home from school, Leah shifted her tote bag from one shoulder to the other and stopped to stare at a dilapidated old house. Everyone said that this was the home of the "Witch of Tall Trees Lane." The small gray bungalow, with its peeling paint and a shutter that dangled off its hinges, was almost hidden because of vines and bushes that grew helter-skelter around it. A loose shingle flapped up and down and a rusty drainpipe lay on the ground. The yard was overgrown with brush, except for a few patches of sandy soil that peeked through the brambles and ivy. The shades were drawn as usual, but Leah always hoped to catch a glimpse of old Mrs. Fox, the supposed witch. The sky darkened and a stillness hung over the house. Leah jumped when a dog barked and an owl screeched. Craning her neck, she looked past a big Keep Out sign to the edge of the cages in back.

She knew they were inhabited by injured animals, which Mrs. Fox sheltered. She took in any abandoned or starving creature that came her way.

The neighbors hated Mrs. Fox, calling her a public nuisance and wishing she'd move. They shunned her, not even saying "good morning." They wanted someone who would mow the lawn and paint the house. Well, Leah thought, pushing back her chestnut hair, Mrs. Fox was doing wonderful work. If Leah could, she'd care for unwanted animals, too. Suddenly there was a movement and the door opened a crack. Rooted to the spot, Leah met two eyes that peered around the corner. When Mrs. Fox caught sight of Leah, she abruptly slammed the door.

Weird, Leah thought, walking on. Suddenly her heart did a flip-flop. Why not interview Mrs. Fox for her English project? She'd find out why she was such a mysterious neighbor. But would Mrs. Fox let her? Leah's steps slowed. She could only try. Mrs. Fox was so unusual. People grumbled about Mrs. Fox, and she sounded scary, but Leah wasn't afraid to interview her. The "witch" might spice up her boring schoolwork.

Later, when Roseanne phoned, Leah excitedly told her about her plan.

"You're going to interview the old witch?" Rose-anne asked in disbelief.

"Tomorrow," Leah answered promptly. "As soon as I finish helping out at the coffee shop."

"Ugh!" Roseanne exclaimed. "You're braver than I'd ever be. She must be a real weirdo. Better watch out. Maybe you should get your dad to go with you."

Leah chuckled. "No, this is *my* interview, and I don't want Miss Calvert accusing me of not doing my own work!"

"You've got a lot of nerve, Leah," Roseanne said. "Call me after you've seen her!"

Leah laughed. "I'll bet she's not as bad as every-one thinks." But secretly she wondered. What was the old saying? Where there's smoke, there's fire. Well, where there's rumors, there's often a reason. What was she letting herself in for? Would Mrs. Fox invite her in for tea? That might be the last of Leah Dvorak!

Leah's step was almost jaunty the next day on the way to see Mrs. Fox. At least the assignment would be interesting! But her heart began to thud fearfully as she approached the porch. Would Mrs. Fox put a spell on her? Was she really a witch? Leah stepped over a broken stair onto a creaking one and for a moment gazed at the forbidding front door. Suddenly a parrot squawked, "Stay out!"

She snapped her head around, her pulse racing. In a cage was a large green parrot whose beady eyes glittered hatefully. Relieved, she said "Hello, Polly," and walked over to the cage. She waggled her fingers playfully outside the wires. "Polly, want a cracker?" she crooned.

"Go away!" screeched the parrot.

Leah giggled. "Mrs. Fox has taught you some very bad manners. Well, Polly, I'm here to see your owner whether you like it or not!"

"Go away!" repeated the parrot. "Stay out!"

Leah laughed softly. "Polly, we're going to be friends."

The parrot cocked his head, rocking to and fro on his perch, but his beak remained shut.

Taking a deep breath, Leah rang the doorbell. While waiting she noticed a fawn tethered off to the side.

"Beautiful baby," she murmured, jumping off the stoop and examining the delicate little deer. She scooped up a handful of straw, and the tan fawn with golden spots gently nibbled on the food.

Leah was so intent on watching the deer that she didn't hear a sound until Mrs. Fox snapped, "What are you doing here? Can't you read? *Keep*

Out means you!" A tiny woman, her brown sun-wrinkled face twisted in a frown, glared at her. The jeans and plaid shirt she had on were worn and faded. Leah saw immediately that the woman wasn't old at all. Mrs. Fox firmly planted her hands on her hips. "You're trespassing, girl!"

"I-I was just giving your deer a snack." She gulped. "Wh-what's his name?"

"*Her* name is Flora!" She pressed her lips together. "As if it's any of your business!"

Leah patted the deer's head and said, "Flora is so beautiful." She bent down, putting her nose close to the fawn's. "Oh," she said in dismay, "her eyes are runny."

"Let's see!" Mrs. Fox said in a worried voice, running down the steps to examine Flora's eyes. "Much better than they were," she muttered. She lifted up Flora's head. "Much better!"

She straightened up, narrowing her eyes at Leah. "Now, young lady, perhaps you'll tell me what you're doing here."

"I came to interview you. It wouldn't take too much of your time —" Briefly Leah explained her English assignment. "Won't you help me?" she pleaded in a low voice.

"I'm not in the habit of inviting strangers in," she said. "Now be off with you!"

Leah's face fell. "I only wanted to talk to you,"

she said, her voice trembling. Mrs. Fox *was* a nasty person. No wonder no one liked her.

But when Mrs. Fox saw Leah's crestfallen face, she softened a bit. "It's not the kind of thing I like to do, but, well, if it's for school . . ." her voice trailed off. "I'm busy now," she continued reluctantly, "but you can come back on Monday."

Leah smiled. "I-I can?" she asked tremulously, not quite believing her good luck.

"I'll be here Monday, right after school," she promised.

"Only for a few minutes," Mrs. Fox warned. "I'm too busy to be answering a lot of fool questions."

"Oh, I won't keep you," she said. But she was eager to talk to Mrs. Fox and maybe even see inside her house.

The next day in Miss Calvert's room Leah told Roseanne all about Mrs. Fox. Roseanne leaned forward, listening intently. "You mean that old woman's not a witch?" she asked in surprise.

Leah laughed. "She's not an old woman. And she's no more a witch than you or me."

"Ha," Roseanne sneered. "I'll bet. Frankly I wouldn't want to meet her on a dark night. I'm afraid she and her black cat would take off on a broomstick."

14

Leah laughed, but for some reason she wished Roseanne and the other kids wouldn't call Mrs. Fox a witch.

"Here's your paper, Leah," Miss Calvert said, handing Leah her English test. "Please see me after class."

Leah nodded, quickly flipping her paper upside down. When no one was looking, she peeked at the comments in red pencil:

Careful of punctuation. You missed the point of this question. You didn't answer the last two questions. Messy. Recopy. See me.

Leah groaned inwardly. She couldn't do anything right. And now she had to listen to another lecture after school. Even if the interview with Mrs. Fox went well, Leah had the feeling that Miss Calvert would still give her a rotten grade. Once you got a reputation as a D student, you were always a D student!

The rest of the day she scarcely heard what was going on, except in science when Mr. Gonser brought in a chameleon and placed it on the lab table. It was fun to see the lizard camouflage itself, changing colors according to the different lights the teacher shined on it.

After school Leah dragged her feet on the way to see Miss Calvert. She was in no hurry for another talk. Standing in the doorway, she watched

Miss Calvert as the tall blonde teacher sat at her desk, intently grading papers. Leah swallowed hard, her palms beginning to sweat. She knew the questions Miss Calvert would ask. And she knew what she'd reply. Yes, she'd try harder. No, she didn't have any problems at home. No, she didn't watch TV all the time. Leah knew by heart the questions teachers asked. And she had the answers down pat, too. Yes, she'd study more. Yes, she'd come in for help.

Leah lifted her small chin. This time she really would apply herself. She had to pass sixth grade. She just had to! If Roseanne and Danielle went to junior high without her, she'd die. Miserably, she cleared her throat.

Miss Calvert glanced up. "Oh, come in, Leah. Please sit down." She leaned back in her chair, folding her arms and gazing at Leah solemnly. "I want to talk to you about your grades."

"I know," Leah mumbled, looking down at her spiral notebook and twisting a loose wire.

Miss Calvert reached for a green folder with Leah's name on it. As she rifled through Leah's written essays and homework, she shook her head. "I'm disappointed in your grades so far, Leah. I'm afraid I'll need to send a warning notice for this marking period."

Leah jerked straight up in her chair. "But-but

it's only the beginning of October," she protested.

"I know, dear, but I don't want your parents to be surprised about your grade when report cards come out."

"They won't be surprised," Leah muttered. Not after all these years, she thought wearily. Her throat tightened and she could hardly breathe. Maybe it was the chalk dust, she told herself. Someone banged a locker in the hall.

"I wanted to go over a few grammar points with you, Leah, and then you can leave."

Leah half-listened to her explanation on the use of the comma. She wanted to meet Roseanne before she got tired of waiting and left.

"Do you understand, Leah?"

Understand what? Leah wondered, but she nodded her head as if she'd been paying attention.

"Then I'll see you tomorrow." The teacher paused. "By the way, I've made an appointment for you to see your counselor. Mrs. Wilcox will see you tomorrow after school."

Leah disgustedly pressed her lips together. The old routine was starting early this year.

"It's for your own good, Leah," Miss Calvert said patiently. "It's very important that you have a good beginning in the sixth grade. This is the first marking period, and I want you to do well." Her bright smile lit up her face.

I'm glad she's so cheerful about my low grades, Leah thought bitterly.

"How's your interview coming?" Miss Calvert rose and threw her pink cardigan around her broad shoulders.

"Wh-what?" she stammered.

"Your interview with the person of your choice. Remember?" She gave Leah a suspicious glance. "You have started on it, haven't you? The outline's due on Monday."

"Oh, yes," Leah answered breezily. "I've got a good start." She didn't really want to discuss Mrs. Fox with Miss Calvert.

"This paper is a very important one," Miss Calvert explained. "I hope you do well. It could salvage your English grade." She hesitated. "Anytime you don't understand something or want help, Leah, my door's always open. I'm here every day until four-thirty."

"Yes, Miss Calvert," Leah answered politely, gathering her books. "And thanks," she called on her way out.

Hurrying to meet Roseanne, she breathed a sigh of relief. One lecture down and one more to go with Mrs. Wilcox.

Roseanne was sitting on the floor, her back to her locker. As usual her nose was stuck in a book. Hearing Leah's heels on the marble floor, she looked up. "Hi!" She scrambled to her feet. "Was Miss Calvert mad?"

"No, she was nice. She gave me the same old baloney about how disappointed she was in my grades." But Leah didn't really want to discuss Miss Calvert and what she'd said. How could Roseanne understand? Kids that got A's would never understand how it felt to get D's. Leah's stomach churned all the way home. Even her enthusiasm for going to the movies with Roseanne on Saturday had vanished.

3

On Saturday morning Leah's parents asked her to help out at The Apple Tree. She was pleased they asked but wondered if they would have if Steven hadn't been off on a camping trip. She was to be in charge of the cash register, since her mom was breaking in a new waitress, and her dad was cooking in the kitchen. It should be easy. She'd done it once before, but not on a Saturday when the coffee shop was the most busy. She loved The Apple Tree's hustle and bustle and the regulars that came in. Just the idea of helping out in the family business filled her with pride. She'd be through by two o'clock — in time to go to the movies with Roseanne.

"Here, Leah," Madeline Dvorak said, handing her an apron, "put this on. We'll need you to help clear away the dirty dishes on the counter." Her blue eyes twinkled, and she gave Leah a bib apron.

"Mo-ther," she protested, reluctantly holding it at arm's length. "Over jeans?"

"Over a lovely pink angora sweater," she retorted.

Leah looked up to the tiled ceiling, but she tied on the white apron.

Madeline Dvorak laughed and gave Leah a hug. "It's great having you here." Dressed in her short red-and-white-checked uniform, with her brown hair tied back, Mrs. Dvorak looked like a young girl to Leah.

"And I like helping, too," Leah said. "Besides, I can use the money."

"Be careful in making change," Madeline warned. "There's a pad and pencil in case you need to do some quick calculations."

"I won't need it," she said confidently. After all, the register gave the amount of change that was due back. What could be easier than that?

The smell of cinnamon buns and hot coffee filled the air of the cozy restaurant, and Leah was all smiles when she greeted the first customer. The cafe was soon filled, and orders flew back and forth between the kitchen and counter. Leah poured cups of coffee and stacked up dirty dishes.

The first man at the cash register was Mr. Schneider. "Everything OK, Mr. Schneider?" she asked, beaming at him and feeling very important.

"Fine, fine," he said, and nodded his head so vigorously that his halo of white hair vibrated in agreement.

After he left, an impatient woman thrust her check at Leah, giving her a twenty-dollar bill. The register screen flashed $17.00 in change. Hastily, Leah counted out a five, two singles, and a twenty. The woman stuffed the money in her purse and hurried out.

Later as she wiped the counter, she stopped abruptly, her forehead breaking out in a cold sweat. What had she done? She'd given that woman a twenty-dollar bill when it should have been a ten! How could she have been so stupid? What good did it do to have the register tell you how much change to give when you pulled the wrong bill? A few more mistakes like that, and instead of being paid for her day's work she'd owe her folks money! She didn't have the courage to tell her mom, but when they totaled up at the end of the day she'd soon find out. Leah decided to confess at the first lull in business.

Somehow she got through the morning, although she was so afraid she'd make another mistake that she felt like a rubber band ready to snap. About eleven the lunch crowd drifted in. Leah had been relieved that her mom hadn't scolded her when she told her about the ten-dollar error. She had just cautioned Leah to be more careful. Sometimes, Leah thought, her mother could be quite understanding.

During the lunch hour a young man handed her a credit card and she had to call her mother over to show her what to do. Mrs. Dvorak placed the card in the machine over the paper form and gave the customer the form to sign.

"I can do it now," Leah said confidently. Leah took in more and more checks and the cash register rang constantly. Several times Leah had punched the wrong key, and her mother had to come to the rescue to void the check. As the lunch crowd thinned one person handed her a credit card. She ran it through the machine but put in the form crooked and jammed it. She groaned silently. Now what? Again she had to call her mom to come over and bail her out.

Taking the next check, Leah glanced up to see a tall man glowering at her. "This is outrageous," he complained peevishly. "I've been standing here ten minutes to pay my bill!"

"Sorry, sir," she said, handing him his change.

"You've shortchanged me a dollar!" he snapped. "What's wrong with you?"

She glanced up at the amount due and saw that he had $6.15 due in change and she'd given him five ones. "I-I miscounted. Sorry," she said in a low voice, her throat tightening as she handed him another dollar. She hoped her mom hadn't heard his bellowing.

"Give me one of those mints!" he ordered harshly.

Nervously, she handed him a wrapped mint and was astonished to see him walk toward the door. "J-just a minute, sir. That will be five cents."

Angrily, he returned and tossed a nickel on the counter. "This is the last time I ever come in here! They need to get a cashier who knows what she's doing!" He spun around and stormed out.

Leah's face burned, and when she tried to smile at the next customer, her underlip trembled so that she had to fight back the tears. Breaking open a package of dimes, Leah's fingers shook so that the coins scattered and rolled beneath the counter and stools.

The customer Leah had overpaid returned, waving a ten-dollar bill. "I thought you'd like to have this back," she said with a smile.

"Oh, yes," Leah breathed. She took the bill and put it in the register. "Thank you so much."

The woman answered pleasantly, "Just count your change carefully after this."

"Oh, I will," Leah promised gratefully as she watched the woman leave.

At last when the door was locked, Leah dropped onto one of the stools. What a mess she'd made of everything!

Her father was soon at her elbow, soothing her. "Well, Leah, I don't know what happened today, but we're $4700 over our usual profit."

"Wh-what?" she stammered.

"You hit the zero key twice," he explained.

"Oh, no," she said miserably. Rising, she slowly untied her apron and hung it on a wall peg. "I'll do better next Saturday," she murmured.

"I'm afraid there won't be a next time for a while, Leah," her mother said gently. "We just can't afford to lose customers or money." She straightened the salt and pepper shakers at each station, then went behind the counter. "Besides, you need your time to study." She lifted a paper cup and peered inside. "Leah!" she gasped, staring at her in dismay. "Where's the newspaper money?"

She slapped her forehead and moaned, "How could I forget?" She knew that all the money from the morning newspapers she sold was supposed to go into the paper cup, clearly marked *Paper*.

Instead she'd rung up each newspaper sale on the cash register. Another dumb mistake. No wonder her dad and mom didn't want her coming back. No one could create more chaos if they'd tried!

"I guess I won't be going to the movies with Roseanne," she said dejectedly.

"You didn't mean to make mistakes," Mr. Dvorak said reassuringly, patting her hand. "It was just a bad day." His square white chef's cap sat jauntily atop his round face, and his rosy cheeks shone like two red apples. "You run along with Roseanne." Smiling, he fished beneath his long apron and gave her enough money for the afternoon.

"Thanks, Dad," she said humbly. It was a wonder he was letting her go to the movies. She felt rotten. It would have been better if he'd yelled at her.

On the way to meet Roseanne, she remembered last year's unit in math on making change, but as usual she hadn't paid much attention. Why hadn't she? Look at all the trouble she caused. Still she knew Monday would be the same old story. She'd be bored with school. Then her heart leaped as she remembered another thing she was to do on Monday — something that wasn't boring. She was going to see Mrs. Fox again. *That* was sure to be interesting!

4

When she reached Roseanne's, Leah noticed the sunlight filtering through the crimson and yellow leaves and the banks of marigolds and asters in front of the green-and-white house. It was a beautiful fall day, but all she could think about was the mess she'd created at The Apple Tree.

Going around to the backyard, Leah stopped to watch Roseanne bouncing up and down on her trampoline. Her fine blonde hair blew around her face like golden streamers.

"Hi, Leah," Roseanne said between bounds. "Come on up! We'll jump together." She sprang higher and higher in the air. Suddenly she somersaulted in midair, landing agilely on her feet. "Hurry up, Leah," she urged.

"We'll be late for the movies," Leah protested.

"Ten minutes."

"OK," Leah said, giving in with a laugh. She

27

kicked off her sneakers and lifted herself onto the frame. She did a flawless forward roll so that she stood facing Roseanne. They leaped and vaulted up to the blue sky. They did full turns, back flips, somersaults, and twirls. The feel of the air whooshing across her flushed face and the exhilarating height made her forget the bungling at the cash register.

As the two breathless girls jumped off the trampoline, Leah once more remembered the grouchy man at The Apple Tree who had said he'd never return. She had actually driven customers away! She turned to tell Roseanne about the day's fiasco, but the words stuck in her throat. How could she confess another stupid thing that she'd done when Roseanne was so perfect?

Suddenly, Roseanne flung her arm around her. "Leah, guess what? I'm having a party a week from Friday." Her violet-blue eyes sparkled. "It starts right after school. Can you come?"

Leah swallowed hard. Roseanne had a way of cheering her up even when she didn't know what was wrong. "I'll be there," she promised and her smile widened. "Is it a dress-up?"

"No, no, it's a scavenger hunt, so wear old clothes."

"Sounds like fun," Leah said, feeling a little

better. Now she had two things to look forward to — Mrs. Fox and the party.

Almost as if she'd heard Leah's thoughts, Roseanne went on. "Maybe, I'll add a fox to the list that everyone will have to get from Mrs. Fox. I hear she keeps hundreds of foxes."

Leah sighed. The stories! The rumors!

"Oh, wouldn't it be neat to put one of her animals on the scavenger list?" Roseanne said excitedly. "I'll bet you'd be the only one that wouldn't get the door slammed on them!"

A faint trickle of fear skidded down Leah's spine. "You can't do that, Roseanne! Mrs. Fox is a very private person and she wouldn't like it if so many kids came banging on the door." Leah paused. "It would scare the animals, too."

Roseanne sniffed. "You act as if you own Mrs. Fox. I'd love to see inside her spooky house and this would be a good way to do it."

"Please, don't," Leah pleaded. "I'm just getting acquainted with her and this could ruin my whole interview."

"Oh, all right," Roseanne said sulkily. "You certainly want to keep her for yourself."

"It isn't that. It-it's hard to explain."

Leah was relieved when they arrived at the movies and the talk about Mrs. Fox ceased. Still, she had a fluttery feeling that Roseanne wouldn't give up until she met Mrs. Fox, and for some reason she was sure they wouldn't hit it off.

Miss Calvert asked to see their outlines for the interviews, but after everything that had happened over the weekend Leah had forgotten to do hers. As a result she got a zero for the day. What a great way to start the week, Leah thought glumly. She should keep an assignment notebook like Roseanne.

After school Miss Calvert stopped her in the hall. "I still need your outline, Leah."

"I'll hand it in tomorrow," she promised glibly.

"Who have you chosen to interview?" Miss Calvert asked.

"Well . . . you'll see . . ." Leah replied cautiously.

"OK, just don't let me down," Miss Calvert said, studying Leah's face. "Did you meet with your counselor?"

"Yes, I saw Mrs. Wilcox," Leah said vaguely. "She said I should get my work in on time and sign up for a tutor."

"Sounds like a good idea."

Leah nodded halfheartedly. Everyone wanted her to spend ninety-nine percent of her time studying. Nuts to that. She had better things to do.

Miss Calvert was a nice person, but Leah felt that, like most teachers, she was too pushy. Of course, she had to admit that Miss Calvert's prodding probably meant she cared and did not intend to let Leah disappear into the woodwork. Even though that was where she'd rather be. Well, she promised herself, she'd definitely write the outline tonight. It would be easy.

"Have a good evening, Leah. I'll look forward to seeing your notes tomorrow." Miss Calvert smiled and opened the door. "Your interview sounds very mysterious. I can't wait to see who your secret person is." Laughing, she left.

Leah stared after her for a long time, wondering if she'd opened a can of worms. Everyone would want to pry into Mrs. Fox's business. And it seemed Mrs. Fox simply wanted to be left alone to care for her animals. Was Leah doing the right thing in writing about her? Yes, she told herself, she was. Otherwise she'd never have gotten to meet her. And today she'd get to find out more about her.

"Leah! Hold on a minute!" Roseanne called.

Leah turned and waited for her. Danielle, hobbling on crutches, was close behind.

When they caught up, Danielle asked, "How's your interview going with the old witch?"

Leah held the door open for her and indignantly replied, "She's not old and she's not a witch!" Boy, once you got a reputation it was hard to shed it! Like being dumb, she suddenly thought. She'd been labeled dumb for as long as she could remember.

"OK, OK," Danielle chortled. "Don't get excited. Why don't you come with me to baseball practice. Of course, all I can do is watch." She kicked up her plaster-encased foot, her round face scrunching into a mock glower. "But it should be interesting. Mary McNee is pitching."

"I can't," Roseanne said. "I've got cheerleading. We're learning a new routine."

"And I'm going to see Mrs. Fox," Leah said defiantly, her small chin rising a notch.

"Ooooohhhh," both girls said in a singsong voice.

Giggling, Roseanne gave a mock shiver. "I hope you come back alive, Leah."

Leah pulled herself up, confronting them. "I will. Don't worry!" she snapped.

Roseanne raised her eyebrows and gave her a quick look. Leah squeezed Roseanne's hand as a way of apologizing, and Roseanne smiled her forgiveness.

"Mrs. Fox seems nice," Leah explained. "Really. You both should get to know her."

"No, thanks," Danielle said, and Roseanne shook her head.

What was the use, Leah thought as she waved good-bye and cut across the schoolyard in the opposite direction.

When she arrived at Mrs. Fox's she walked briskly up to the front door and rang the bell. When the parrot fastened a beady eye on her and screamed, "Go away," she only chuckled. This time she was prepared!

"Go away, yourself, Polly" she answered saucily. "You'd better get used to me 'cause I plan to visit here often!"

"Oh, you do, do you?" Mrs. Fox said, flinging wide the door. She folded her arms across her chest, looking sternly at Leah.

Leah gulped and gave Mrs. Fox a slight smile. The petite woman wore jeans again, but this time she had on an oversized sweater rolled up to her elbows.

"Well, ask your questions," she commanded, "I'm a busy person." Leah took out her pad and pencil, wishing Mrs. Fox would invite her in. It was chilly out on the porch. But after they had talked a bit, Leah was relieved when Mrs. Fox agreed to let her return and talk some more the following day.

And for the next few days, Leah did all her interviewing outdoors. She found out, though, that Mrs. Fox wasn't mean. She was gruff, didn't waste time, and was impatient with inefficient people, but she clearly liked how tenderly Leah treated her animals. If only Leah could gain her trust and prove to her that she, too, cared about the work Mrs. Fox was doing.

On the fifth day, Mrs. Fox opened her door wide, and her face cracked into a small smile. "I can see you like animals." She shook a finger under Leah's nose. "I think you'd like my dog, Ozzie." She motioned her forward, bounding up the steps. "Follow me!"

Leah's heart leaped. She was going into the mysterious house!

With a racing pulse, Leah stepped gingerly into the gloomy room, her nose wrinkling immediately at the strong smell of disinfectant. Cages lined the walls, some with animals, others empty. Lace curtains, yellow with age, drooped at the windows, and an old brown wicker rocker was in the middle of the threadbare rug. Stacks of books and papers were piled in a nearby basket. One couch and one floor lamp completed the living room furniture.

Mrs. Fox went into the dining room. "Come in, come in," she said impatiently. "Don't dawdle." Leah stood as if transfixed, then carefully followed her, not touching anything.

The paint might be flaking off the walls and the wooden floors splintery, but the cages were scrubbed clean. A round oak table on a heavy pedestal, encircled by four wooden chairs, dominated the center of the room, but what caught Leah's eye was a breakfront with a glass door. The inside shelves were filled with foxes: glass foxes, clay foxes, and wooden foxes, red foxes, silver foxes, black foxes, and gray foxes. And on the wall were paintings of foxes.

Mrs. Fox chuckled. "Because of my name, on every holiday someone gives me a fox or two. Pretty soon foxes will take over the house. But," she said, stooping over a large cage, "here's a real fox. I came upon this little fellow last week in a trap."

Leah bent down, too, and a bright little fox gazed back at her, full of curiosity. His right foreleg was bandaged, but other than that, he appeared alert and healthy.

"Edgar's ready for me to drive him back out to the hills. His paw's almost healed."

"Oh," Leah said eagerly, "could I go with you?"

Mrs. Fox gave her a strange look, but before she could reply a cocker spaniel wagged its way into the room.

"Ozzie!" Mrs. Fox said. "Come and meet . . . ?" She hesitated, giving Leah a quizzical look. "What's your name again, girl?"

"Leah," she answered, bending down and holding out her hands to Ozzie. "Leah Dvorak."

"Well, Leah, meet Ozzie."

The black curly-haired dog, wiggling his whole body, licked eagerly at Leah's fingers, then her face. "Sweet dog. Sweet Ozzie," she cooed, nuzzling the pup's neck. "I'd love to take you home, fella."

"I couldn't give Ozzie away," Mrs. Fox said, shaking her head. "Ozzie and I are attached to one another."

"My mom's allergic so we don't have any animals." Leah looked up at Mrs. Fox. "She wouldn't let me have a dog anyway. Y-You see my grades aren't too good and . . ." her voice trailed off.

"I understand," Mrs. Fox said briskly. "But I can see you're a very caring person."

"I'd be a good pet owner," she answered, flattered by Mrs. Fox's comment. She bent down and scratched one of Ozzie's floppy ears. And if she could have a dog like him, she'd give him a good home — a very good home. She sighed wistfully.

But since she couldn't have a pet, it would mean a lot to her to visit Mrs. Fox and her animals.

"Come," Mrs. Fox said in a matter-of-fact tone, "meet the rest of my menagerie." She gave Ozzie a pat as she went by.

"What was wrong with Ozzie?" Leah asked, trailing after her. "Did you take him in because he was sick?"

"The pup wasn't sick," she said grimly. "Someone just pushed him out of their car." She pointed across the road. "Over there by the woods. I saw the whole thing. I ran after them, but they went roaring off before I could even get their license plate number. Can you imagine anyone doing such a thing? The poor abandoned puppy ran after the car, completely bewildered. He whimpered when I picked him up, but he adjusted fast enough.

"He's had a lot of love ever since. Of course he has to share his home with Mr. McTavish, the parrot, Flora, the deer, Jack, the raccoon, and Frank, the woodchuck. Plus my two cats," she paused, studying Leah's face, "Sima and Willie, who will be asleep on the kitchen chairs."

Dutifully, Leah followed Mrs. Fox. She planned to write the best English essay she'd ever written. Of course she'd never gotten above a D in English, but with this assignment she felt things were looking up. She really wanted to write about the wonderful work Mrs. Fox was doing. If she could only make that come across in her writing! She already had a good idea how she'd start it. In her mind's eye she wrote the words:

When I came up the steps to see Mrs. Fox, known as "The Witch of Tall Trees Lane," the first words I heard were, "Stay out." It wasn't Mrs. Fox, though. It was her guard-parrot.

She smiled to herself. Yes, she had an idea this would be the best paper she'd ever written.

"Come into the kitchen," Mrs. Fox ordered, "and have a seat. Chase Sima away. That cat thinks she owns the window chair." Her deep voice was clipped and to the point, but Leah thought her abruptness was only a front.

"Scoot," Leah said to a gorgeous silver-haired Persian that was curled up comfortably on the chair cushion. The cat opened one sleepy yellow eye but didn't budge.

Gently she lifted the cat and set her down on the floor, where the cat sat, her front paws daintily together, and stared reproachfully at Leah.

"Sorry, friend," Leah said, reaching down and tickling the cat's ear. Sima, however, refused to be pacified and stalked away, tail high and waving like a silver plume.

Mrs. Fox began making tea. "I've told you enough about me for a while," she said. "Why don't you tell me a little about yourself?"

Before she knew it, Leah was telling her all about herself. She even told Mrs. Fox about Saturday's cash register disaster. Somehow she sensed Mrs. Fox would understand. She wondered how she could confide in this stranger when she hadn't been able to tell her best friend. But Mrs. Fox didn't seem like a stranger. She seemed like someone Leah had known all her life.

5

Leah finished her tea and took out paper and a pencil. "May I ask you some more questions, Mrs. Fox?"

Mrs. Fox raised her eyebrows. "Anything to get you a passing grade, Leah. Fire away, but I'm sure I've already told you everything."

Leah grinned. "I think there's a lot left to tell. You'd be surprised how many people are interested in you." Seeing Mrs. Fox's brief frown, she quickly asked, "How long have you cared for animals?"

"Oh, forever," Mrs. Fox said. "I'm forty-six years old, and as long as I can remember I've always loved animals. I really learned about them when I grew up on a farm in Iowa. In high school I worked as a veterinarian's assistant."

Leah wrote furiously while Mrs. Fox picked up Ozzie, giving him a hug. The cocker spaniel licked her hands, then settled down in a round furry bundle on her lap.

Leah reached over, scratching Ozzie's ears. The curly-haired pup lifted his head, then contentedly buried it between his paws and closed his eyes. What a pretty picture, she thought. "Mrs. Fox," she asked, suddenly having a brainstorm, "would you mind if I took some photos of you and your animals?"

Mrs. Fox hesitated, then shrugged. "I guess not. But this is only for your English teacher's eyes, right?"

"Right," answered Leah, pleased at her idea. That should help explain what Mrs. Fox did, and when Miss Calvert saw the lovable animals she'd be taken in, too. Leah glanced around the kitchen. The wooden cupboards were chipped and the linoleum worn, but everything was spotlessly clean. When she'd come in, she'd noticed a portrait of a man and a young boy about her age. She yearned to ask who they were, but something held her back. She didn't want to pry into Mrs. Fox's personal life.

"You have a great set-up here, Mrs. Fox, but isn't it expensive to care and feed all these animals?"

"Yes," Mrs. Fox said dryly, gently stroking Ozzie's back, "but I have a small pension, and I don't need much to live on." She hesitated. "Oh, there are a few things I'd like to fix. My house needs a new roof and a coat of paint. I'd like to put in a dog run, but that will have to wait."

"How long have you lived here?"

"Since before you were born, Leah. Fifteen years. According to my neighbors, that's fifteen years too long. Nothing would please them more than to see me move." She pressed her lips together. "But I have as much right to my life-style as they do to theirs."

"Why do they want you to leave?" Leah asked. "You do such good work."

She barked a short, harsh laugh. "Not if you heard them talk! My lawn isn't a green carpet — I have cages stuck here and there — I feed the pigeons — my house needs repair. I could go on and on, but you get the idea. In other words, Blanche Fox is a public nuisance." She shook her head. "I don't bother anyone, but it would be nice," she said wistfully, "if someone said 'good morning' once in a while."

Poor Mrs. Fox, Leah thought. She must feel so alone. Even if she didn't crave company, it would give her a sense of security to be able to call someone in an emergency. What if there were a fire? Or what if she got sick? A knot formed in Leah's stomach. It was a rotten way to treat a neighbor. The Dvoraks were part of the neighborhood, too. Her parents were kind, but they didn't know much about Mrs. Fox. And Leah had to admit she hadn't either until she got this assignment.

Mrs. Fox set Ozzie down and stood up. A few wisps of hair had loosened from her braids, and she impatiently brushed them back. She looked like a young woman with a slender, firm body and lively green eyes. What made people think she was old? Perhaps it was because they had only caught a distant glimpse of her. Maybe it was because they'd seen a small, tanned face with deep crevices due to the sun. Others, like Roseanne, had never seen her up close but just assumed she was old.

Leah watched Mrs. Fox pour water into Ozzie's bowl and longed to say something comforting, but the lump in her throat prevented her. She rose and examined the titles of the books on the counter. She smiled. Most kitchens had cookbooks, but these books were about dog care, cat care, rabbit care, and bird feeders. She took more notes for her paper.

"Want to borrow any of those books?" Mrs. Fox asked gruffly.

"Could I?" Leah scanned the titles, wondering which one to take.

"Sure, take this one on dogs." Mrs. Fox pulled out a tattered book and handed it to her. "You'll learn how pups like Ozzie should be cared for."

Gratefully, Leah tucked the book into her tote bag.

"Anything you don't understand, just ask me," Mrs. Fox said.

"I'd like that." Leah reluctantly stood up to leave. She was excited about Monday, though, when she'd return. Mrs. Fox planned to set Edgar, the fox, free and had invited her along.

After the weekend, on her way to Mrs. Fox's, Leah thought of how unhappy Roseanne had been when Leah wouldn't go with her to the mall. But right now Mrs. Fox was first on her list. Especially since they were taking Edgar to North River Woods. Leah smiled, thinking how happy the fox would be to be let loose. Leah was also pleased because she'd received a B on her outline. Miss Calvert said it would have been an A, but because it was a day late it was marked down a grade. Even so, she'd gotten a B! She couldn't remember the last time she'd seen such a high mark. And if her paper had been on time she would have received her first A! It was unbelievable! Already, without even knowing it, Mrs. Fox had helped her.

Hurrying up the walk, Leah broke into a run when she saw Mrs. Fox trying to lift Edgar's crate. She grabbed one end of the box. Mrs. Fox looked up, surprised, but when she saw Leah she smiled. Together they pushed Edgar's box into the back of the pickup. The truck was rusted, its red paint was peeling, and it had a few dents, but it appeared sturdy and serviceable.

"Thanks, Leah. Let's get our little friend out to the woods where he can run free." Mrs. Fox turned the ignition key and they were off, heading down the bumpy gravel road toward the banks of the North River.

Bouncing along the tree-lined road, Leah said casually, "I got a B on my outline today."

Mrs. Fox glanced at her, and a half-smile lit her dark face. "I guess that proves something, Leah. You can do it."

"It felt good," she admitted.

"Have you started to read that dog-care book?"

"Yes, but there were a lot of words I didn't understand."

"Did you bring it along?"

Leah nodded.

"When we get back we can talk over anything you have questions about."

"I'd like that," Leah said, leaning back on the seat.

Arriving at the river's edge, Blanche Fox stopped the truck, and together she and Leah hauled out the crate. Edgar peered out between the mesh wires, yipping excitedly. Mrs. Fox leaned down and yanked open the cage door. "Come on, old friend," she coaxed softly. "You're home."

No more urging was necessary. Edgar dashed out and raced up a small hill. The red fox stopped once, sniffing the air. He turned and stared at them for an instant, then with a low whine he scampered into the brush and disappeared.

Leah's throat constricted. Thanks to Mrs. Fox, another animal had been nursed back to health. She yearned to be just like her. Suddenly, she knew what she wanted to do with her life. More than anything else in the world, she wanted to care for animals, too. She wondered how smart you had to be to become a veterinarian. Her jaw tightened. No matter how much studying it took, she'd do it. Steven wasn't the only one who knew what he wanted to be!

6

On the following day Leah brought another list of questions from the dog-care book: mostly about words that she didn't understand, like *constitute, ointment, hock, withers, flank, dewlap,* and *heelknob*. She and Mrs. Fox sat at the kitchen table going over the words.

Soon, however, Blanche Fox stood up, handing her a dictionary. "You look up the last three, Leah, while I feed Sima and Willie."

Although Leah seldom used a dictionary, she laboriously wrote out the definitions, determined to memorize each one. If she planned to be a veterinarian, then she'd better know these terms.

While Mrs. Fox mixed up mash with some dry food, Leah brushed and combed Ozzie's black coat. The fall day was chilly, but the kitchen was cozy and warm. The oven was on, and the smell of baking bread filled the air.

After she'd finished grooming Ozzie, Leah gave

him a hug. Exuberantly, Ozzie attempted to lick her face, but she laughingly set him down.

"I brought my camera," Leah said hesitantly, not knowing if Mrs. Fox really meant to give her permission to take pictures.

"Go ahead. Click away," Mrs. Fox responded, setting two bowls on a sheet of clean newspaper.

Both cats came running. Sima, the silver-haired Persian, daintily ate from one bowl while Willie dug into his as if someone were ready to pounce on it.

Leah snapped several pictures from different angles, then visited the cages on the closed-in porch, photographing each animal.

Going into the living room, she took several flash photos of Mr. McTavish perched on the swing in his corner bird cage.

"Go away!" he screeched.

"All right, all right," she agreed finally, glancing around the room to see what else to take. She paused at the picture of the man with the young boy and picked up the frame to examine their faces. The man wasn't handsome, but he had gentle eyes and a pleasant smile. However, it was the grinning boy who caught her eye. He had dark spiky hair and a missing front tooth, and his full face was dotted with even more freckles than Leah had.

"That was my husband, Mike, and my son, Jamie," Mrs. Fox explained quietly, entering the room and sitting in the rocker.

Leah returned the picture to the end table, not knowing what to say. The parrot screeched. Then all she heard was the ticking clock. Finally, Leah found her voice. "They look nice."

Mrs. Fox nodded. "They were nice," she said simply.

"What happened to them?" Leah asked in a small voice.

"They drowned in a fishing boat accident fifteen years ago." Mrs. Fox reached over and ran her rough hand over the picture glass. "They were on Lake Lakota when a wind squall came up and swamped their boat, overturning it."

Sitting with her hands folded in her lap, Mrs. Fox stared out the window. She ran her tongue over her lips. "I left Iowa shortly after the accident and bought this place. I wanted to find an area where I didn't know a soul and where there wouldn't be so many painful reminders." A smile flickered across her craggy features. "Nothing, however, can erase my memories.

"Jamie was similar to you, Leah. I suppose he was like any ordinary ten-year-old, but to me he was special. He was especially kind and gentle with animals. Full of energy, too. Maybe that was

49

why he was always willing to pitch in and help Mike and me with the farm work on our small acreage. After — after — the drowning," her voice cracked and she visibly swallowed, gazing at Leah. "Sorry," she said, "it's still difficult to speak of him."

"Oh, Mrs. Fox," Leah said, impulsively placing her hand on her shoulder. "You don't need to talk about it anymore."

"No-no, I want to," Blanche Fox answered, reaching up and patting Leah's hand. "I haven't shared my feelings with anyone for years. It helps to talk about it with someone who cares."

Leah felt her heart squeezed in anguish.

Mrs. Fox continued. "I remember once when Jamie and I went berry picking, and he got stung by a wasp. He tried not to cry, but suddenly he dashed into my arms for me to comfort him. He was such a brave little boy. So brave . . ." her voice trailed off.

The two sat in silence for a long while. The light began to fade and finally Leah stood up. "I guess I'd better get home. I'll be back tomorrow."

"Fine, Leah." Mrs. Fox rose, too, and quickly brushed away a tear. Then she blew her nose and drew back her shoulders. "It's time to feed Flora."

Together they went out the back door.

"See you tomorrow," Mrs. Fox said, heading

toward the shed where the deer was kept. Then she stopped and turned back toward Leah. "I always look forward to your visits," she added. Leah watched her disappear into the shed, then halted briefly at the duck pond. Several mallards dived and swam over the weed-choked water. She ached for Mrs. Fox and her loss. The mallard hen quacked when she turned and went out the gate.

All the way home Leah thought about what had happened to Mrs. Fox's husband, Mike, and her son, Jamie. How awful. It was a good thing Mrs. Fox had her animals.

She was so lost in thought that she didn't see Roseanne and Danielle until they were almost on top of her.

"Leah, you missed seeing Danielle hobbling around on the softball field today. She managed to throw the ball around a little bit. And now only two weeks till the cast comes off," Roseanne said. "We walked over to Michelini's Drug Store and had a soda to celebrate. Danielle, of course, had to have her usual chocolate fix, too." She laughed, and once Danielle had balanced herself on her crutches, Roseanne handed over the ice cream cone she'd been holding.

Danielle licked the chocolate ice cream and chuckled. "This ruins the old diet, but I'll never give up chocolate."

Roseanne narrowed her eyes. "Where were you, Leah?"

Danielle, taking another swipe at her cone, stopped. "Where else? I'll bet you were at Mrs. Fox's, right, Leah?"

Leah glanced at Roseanne, almost hating to admit it. Why did she feel guilty when they taunted her about Mrs. Fox? "Yes," she admitted in a low voice. "I took some pictures for my interview." She wouldn't, couldn't tell them how Mrs. Fox had confided in her.

Danielle munched on the last of her cone. "You've been at Mrs. Fox's every afternoon," she accused. "One of these days you're going to have to save some time for us!"

"I'm glad our paper is due next week," Roseanne said. "Then we'll be together again." Her clear blue eyes focused intently on Leah. "Won't we?" she asked.

"Sure, we will," Leah answered, but she knew she wouldn't completely give up visiting Mrs. Fox.

"What's that?" Roseanne questioned, catching sight of the book Leah had tucked under her arm.

"It's a book on dog care," Leah replied, hugging the new book closer to her side.

Roseanne laughed. "You don't have time for

your schoolwork, but you read any old book the witch hands you."

Leah indignantly threw back her shoulders. "I've asked you not to call her that, Roseanne."

"Pardon me," Roseanne said sweetly. "I forgot. Is 'the old crone' better?"

Leah angrily brushed past them. Maybe if she introduced them to Mrs. Fox they'd learn to like her as much as she did, but she had her doubts.

Hanging up her jacket in the hall closet, Leah went into the living room where Steven was seated in an easy chair before the fireplace. He glanced up from his book. "Did Mrs. Fox finally let you come home?"

"Ummmhmmm," she answered, dropping in the chair opposite him. The crackling blaze felt good. "Where's Mom and Dad?"

"The O'Connors invited them for supper. Mom left sauerkraut and bratwurst for us."

"I'm not hungry."

Steven got up and placed his sturdy hands on the fireplace mantle, staring into the crackling flames. "What's *with* you lately? You're never home — you're never hungry — you're even reading a book!" He gave her a sidelong look. "You're not sick, are you?"

She laughed lightly. "No, I'm not sick, Steven."

Then her smile faded. "Oh, Steven. It's Mrs. Fox. I feel so sorry for her." And she told her brother the whole story.

For a while Steven continued to gaze at the orange fire. "I guess we're lucky, Leah. We've got our family." His gray eyes shone silver in the firelight. "I've even got a pretty good little sister."

"And I've got a pretty good big brother. Even if he's a pain at times," Leah teased. "Steven," she blurted out, "I'm going to be a vet."

"You're eleven years old for Pete's sake, Leah. How could you possibly know what you want to be?" Steven said with a laugh.

"I just know," she answered calmly. "You're not the only one who can decide on a career."

"I'll bet you change your mind ten times before you're a freshman in high school." He gave her a superior smile.

Not replying, she merely smiled back. She knew as sure as her name was Leah Dvorak that she had chosen the only possible career for herself.

7

On Friday Leah hurried to Roseanne's, thinking how much fun the scavenger hunt would be. She'd miss seeing Mrs. Fox today, though. As she walked along Tall Trees Lane, a few crimson leaves drifted across her face. She felt pretty in her checkered red-and-black top and black jeans and had taken extra pains with her shoulder-length hair. She brushed it until it shone like brown satin and curled softly around her face. She loved how it swished silkily against her ears.

When she arrived, all the kids were there. Danielle was chomping on a chocolate bar and listening to Mike Dunn. Mrs. Fairbanks had set out hot chocolate for everyone while Roseanne handed out Xeroxed lists of instructions. Nat Jenkins, Jason Ross, and Terry O'Bannion were huddled in a corner whispering and laughing. Leah wondered what they were cooking up now as she slipped in next to Andrea White. Two other classmates,

Barbara Franken and Neal Schultz, made a total of nine participants in the hunt.

"Now listen everyone," Roseanne said. "No one is to have a partner. You're on your own. There will be two prizes, a first prize and a booby prize, and the first one back with everything on the list wins."

Roseanne went on, "I'll be here when you return to check off your list. You should finish before it gets dark and in time for supper."

"What's on the menu?" Danielle asked, crumpling up her candy wrapper.

Mike made a fist, hitting her lightly on the arm. "You would ask that!"

Roseanne grinned. "Danielle, you're more interested in the food than the hunt."

"That's true," Danielle admitted amiably. "Where's my list? I should get a head start since I'm still thumping around on a cast."

"You're faster than most of us with two good legs," Mike protested.

Danielle grinned in answer as if she knew she could outdo anyone when it came to speed.

Leah quickly scanned the directions. A map and a list of the following items was on the sheet:

a stuffed fish
Raggedy Ann doll

porcelain dog
Sears catalogue
duck decoy
world atlas
red pen
lemon squeezer
white candle
a Christmas wreath

Since she was usually last in school marks, she'd love to be first in the hunt.

Roseanne smiled at Leah, and she smiled back. She was relieved that their quarrel over Mrs. Fox was forgotten. She needed her friends. Yet, she thought, she was beginning to need Mrs. Fox, too.

"OK, everyone," Roseanne said in a loud voice. "We're about to start. Look at the street addresses. There will be houses with porch lights on which will help you find certain items. With other things you're on your own."

Leah examined the map and looked at the first item on the list. A stuffed fish, she thought in dismay. Where in the world would she find that!

Roseanne looked at her Swatch watch. "OK, gang, take off. And good luck!"

Leah raced out the door and headed for North Third Avenue. She was way ahead of everyone else, which she hoped meant she would finish first.

She looked at the houses along the street, but not one had a porch light turned on. Maybe they'd forgotten.

She rapped on the door of a corner house. "Do you have a stuffed fish?" she asked the man who answered the door.

"Very funny!" he snarled, slamming the door in her face.

Not a very good start, she thought, slowly going down the walk. Then her pace picked up as she rushed from one house to another. Before she knew it she was on Fourth Street. She doubled back to Third. The map *said* Third Street. But everything was so quiet! Not one house had a welcoming light.

Again in the twilight she studied the map. She'd wasted a lot of time and hadn't found the first item! Suddenly she peered at the map more closely. She shouldn't be on *North* Third Street! She should be on *South* Third Street. How many blocks away was that?

She began to run, but when she got to South Third Street, the porch lights were off here, too. She was bewildered. This stupid map wasn't right! Then she saw a porch light in the center of the block and made a dash toward it.

Knocking on the door, Leah was greeted by a

tall, white-haired woman. She thrust the list at her, asking breathlessly, "Do you have any items on this list?"

The woman looked first at her, then at the list, handing it back. "I did have several things," she said in a puzzled tone, "but other kids claimed them a long time ago. You'd better hurry and catch up. It's getting dark."

Not bothering to answer, Leah flew down the porch steps and ran to the corner. A raindrop splattered against her cheek. Pulling up her collar, she grimaced at the threatening sky. A bolt of lightning zigzagged across the black clouds. She shivered.

Standing under a street lamp, she wondered which way to go. She remembered the map said "Greenwood Street." That was only two blocks away, so off she ran again. It was pitch dark now, and a steady rain pelted her face. Her heart pounded. She hadn't found one item.

On Greenwood Street, she looked up and down the block. She was confused. There were no porch lights, and black shadows surrounded her! What should she do? She couldn't return dragging an empty tote bag. She wouldn't. She knocked on several doors, and one man was kind enough to rummage around until he produced a white candle. Knocking on four more doors she was finally lucky enough to find someone with a Sears catalogue.

But two items were all she could find. A dog barked, scaring her. No one was on the street. She was all alone. An icy knot formed in her stomach. Where was she? If she was lost, she'd be the laughingstock of Roseanne's party. Well, she would find her way back! She yanked the map out of her pocket and tried to read the smudged directions.

Oh, no, she muttered. The map said Greenwood *Avenue*, not Greenwood *Street*. How dumb! Why hadn't she read the map more carefully? She had no idea how to get back to Tall Trees Lane. She was really lost. She wandered up and down the desolate street.

At last, biting her trembling underlip, she bravely went up to a house and asked how to get to Tall Trees Lane. She was only six blocks away — not as far as she'd thought. Six blocks in the darkness, though, seemed more like six miles. She pressed her hand over her mouth and fought back the tears. Throwing the tote bag over her shoulder, she felt the weight of the Sears catalogue. She hurried as fast as she could.

At last she reached Tall Trees Lane. Now she knew where she was. Never had she been so happy to see the familiar houses on her street.

Arriving at Roseanne's house, she took the steps two at a time. When she burst into the living room, where everyone was having dinner, she realized what a mess she was. Embarrassed, she stood facing everyone with a dirty face, her shirt hanging limply outside her jeans and her once softly curled hair drooping in wet strands.

Roseanne jumped up, putting down her plate. "Leah," she said with concern, "where have you been?"

"All over town," she said ruefully.

"We were worried," Mrs. Fairbanks said, offering her a hot dog.

Leah bit into the cold frankfurter. Everyone else had finished eating, and here she was just beginning.

Terry O'Bannion chuckled. "You look like you got hit by a truck, Leah. What'd you do? Misread the map?"

She nodded, the bun sticking to the roof of her mouth like a soggy piece of cotton. If only she'd paid closer attention to the map and to geography. North was always up on a map and South always down. No wonder she had gotten lost. Why hadn't she remembered that? She put down her half-eaten hot dog.

Roseanne presented her with a wrapped box.

"You won the booby prize," she said, a lilt in her voice.

Leah managed a twisted smile as she untied the ribbon and thought, why am I always the one to win the booby prize?

She lifted out a small compass to the good natured laughter all around her.

"You sure can use that, Leah," Mike Dunn boomed. "Now maybe you can find your way home."

Laughter rang in Leah's ears, and she blushed furiously. She'd been so looking forward to this party, and now she couldn't wait for it to end!

8

By Monday morning the embarrassment of the party had almost disappeared from Leah's mind. But as soon as she walked through the doors of John Adams School, the unpleasant feeling came flooding back.

Mike Dunn, ambling down the hall with Danielle, called out to Leah, "How many times *did* you get lost going home Friday night?"

Her answering laugh curdled in her mouth, and she felt her face turn hot pink.

Danielle turned to smooth things over. "Don't pay any attention to Mr. Perfect, Leah. He should crow! Remember the time he fell through the ice on Miller's Pond?" Her close-set eyes squinted with mirth. "Not too smart, Mr. Dunn."

"Oh, yeah?" he said, giving Danielle a light shove. Forgetting Leah, they walked on, continuing their mock battle. "And, Danielle," Mike said in a loud voice, "what about the time you dived into . . ."

Leah spun about and hurried into class. Her ears were still burning when she took her seat in Miss Calvert's room.

Standing before her desk, Miss Calvert announced, "First of all, I want you all to remind your parents about the Open House tonight."

Miss Calvert's soft dark eyes seemed to bore directly into hers. Open House, Leah moaned silently. What new horror would Mom and Dad learn about her schoolwork? Despite the B she'd earned on her outline, her grades were still low. What could one B do against ten D's and F's? Would she be grounded again?

"Class, please pass your interviews to the front of the room," Miss Calvert said. "I'm looking forward to reading them. Your outlines were excellent so I know your reports will be good." Gathering the papers from the first student in each row, she looked directly at Leah and gave her a special smile.

Leah smiled back. For the first time she wasn't ashamed of what she'd written. It was good. She knew it. She hoped Miss Calvert wouldn't take too long to grade them. For once she was eager to have a paper returned.

However, when Miss Calvert handed back her history homework, she wasn't at all eager to see this grade. After a quick glance at her paper, Leah turned it over. She didn't want anyone else to glimpse the big red D at the top. Although she'd known her grade would be low because she'd only answered six of the ten study questions, she'd still hoped for a C.

Her spirits sunk even lower when it was time for geography. Terry O'Bannion turned around, opening his book to a map of Europe. "This is north," he whispered, pointing to Norway, "and this is south." He indicated boot-shaped Italy. "This is east," he teased and pointed at Russia. "This is west." He tapped his forefinger on France. "Get it?" He grinned, his black eyes twinkling.

She wanted to hit him over the head with her book. Instead she glanced at Roseanne, who was shaking her head at Terry in mock disapproval. But a small smile played around her lips.

Fine, Leah thought bitterly, burying her head in the oversized book. My dumbness is always good for a laugh.

After school Roseanne quickly caught up with Leah. "Let's go to Michelini's for a Coke," she said, threading her arm through Leah's.

Leah stiffened. She dreaded turning Roseanne down again. Swallowing hard, she said, "I'm sorry, Roseanne, but I promised Mrs. Fox I'd help clean cages. Maybe tomorrow?"

"Just forget it!" Roseanne snapped, planting her hands on her hips. "Tomorrow I have cheerleading practice." She glared at Leah. "I'm tired of asking you and asking you to do things. Both Danielle and I have had it." She paused dramatically. "If you ever have a spare moment, let me know!" She stalked off, turning to give Leah a last scornful look. "Do you know what they call you, Leah? The Witch's Assistant, that's what!"

"I don't care!" Leah shouted back. "I don't care!" But she did care. She cared a lot.

When she arrived, Mrs. Fox greeted her crisply, "Glad you're here, Leah." Her sweatshirt sleeves were pushed up, and she was holding a bowl of cat food. She handed it to Leah. "Look what the animal control boys just dropped off." A large gray cat huddled in a corner, gazing at her with dull green eyes.

Leah went right over to the thin cat. "Poor baby," she crooned. "You look like you haven't been fed for days." She put the bowl of food down next to the water bowl. The starved cat began to eat ravenously. "Is it a he or she?" she queried, turning to Mrs. Fox.

"She's a she," Mrs. Fox answered. She stroked the cat's scraggly coat. "Leah will have you waltzing around in no time, Cat."

"Waltzing," Leah murmured. Her eyes lit up. "We learned about World War II songs in fifth grade, and one of the songs was called 'Waltzing Matilda' from Australia. Let's call her Matilda," Leah said, half-questioningly.

Mrs. Fox nodded. "Matilda, it is. I just hope I can find a good home for her. I can't have three cats plus all my other animals."

Leah brought a clean flannel blanket from the closet and placed it in a large cardboard box. She gently put shivering Matilda in the box when she'd finished eating. The cat snuggled into the blanket and fell fast asleep.

Leah grabbed a bucket and a brush and set to work, scrubbing out the cages. Ozzie bounced in and ran to Mrs. Fox, then to Leah.

"Shoo, Ozzie. We have work to do." Mrs. Fox threw a toy bone, and the exuberant puppy chased after it, skittering and sliding across the bare floor. Soon, however, he was back for more. Giving a throaty laugh, Mrs. Fox scratched Ozzie's floppy ears. "I don't know what I'd do without this little fellow," she said warmly. "He's my buddy." She sank back on her haunches, and Ozzie placed a paw on her knee, gazing earnestly into her face. "He's a special dog — one I could never part with."

Leah chuckled. "He's a lot of company for you."

"Sure is. After Beezer, my German shepherd, died two years ago, I've wanted another dog." She nuzzled Ozzie. "But it had to be the right one, a dog I could love as much as Beezer."

Leah was happy to see Mrs. Fox and Ozzie together. They were a perfect team. But Mrs. Fox needed to have people around, too. All at once she realized what she could do to bring cheer into Mrs. Fox's dreary life. "Could you come to dinner sometime?" she said, excitement bubbling over in her voice. "Mom and Dad would like to meet you." And knowing how kind her parents were, she was sure they'd welcome Mrs. Fox into their home.

One eyebrow shot up and Mrs. Fox said in a dry tone, "*They* want to meet me? Or do *you* want them to meet me?" She smiled. "You mean well, Leah, but, no, I don't think so. I'm content to stay here." She looked around at her animals. "I've got all the friends I need right here." She resumed scrubbing the bird cage. "For fifteen years I've been alone with just my animals, Leah, and I've grown accustomed to it."

Disappointed, Leah also resumed her scrubbing. She'd like to introduce her friend around the neighborhood, but if Mrs. Fox didn't want to, what could she do?

"It's just that I've chosen to live this way," Mrs. Fox said, noticing Leah's unhappy face. "The neighbors hate me and prefer that I keep my distance. It's a little late to be reaching out."

"They don't hate you," Leah protested. "They just don't know you. If they knew you like I do," she added shyly, "they'd want to visit you often."

Mrs. Fox chuckled. "I have a good life here, and I don't want to change. Come," she said, getting off her knees. "It's time for a cup of coffee."

Coffee? Leah thought. How delicious. She wasn't allowed coffee at home, but when Mrs. Fox set the steaming mug before her and she tasted it, she was surprised how sweet and creamy it was.

"It's half sugar and half milk with a little coffee," Mrs. Fox told her.

"It's wonderful," Leah remarked.

"Time for vocabulary drill," Mrs. Fox said. "Any new words today?"

"Lots," Leah responded with a grin, pulling out a list and laying it on the table.

Together they went over the words, and the

afternoon flew by. Leah basked in the feeling that Mrs. Fox genuinely seemed to enjoy her company. Before she left, Leah took a few more snapshots, even though her paper had been turned in. These would be just for her. For starters, she snapped the miniature fox collection and the new sleeping Matilda.

That night she was lying on the floor in front of the TV with a book propped up in front of her, but not really studying. Steven had popped popcorn, and it was a nice evening, although she dreaded her parents' return from Open House. Maybe it wouldn't be as bad as she thought.

At nine when her mom and dad came in, their faces grim, Leah knew that it was as bad as she'd expected.

"Leah," Jan Dvorak said, hanging up his trench coat, "come into the kitchen. We want to talk to you." So, Leah thought gloomily, following him and Mom into the other room, she was due for another lecture.

"Leah, Miss Calvert told us about your homework," her father said. "Your grades are slipping." His round face was serious. "I think you're spending too much time at Mrs. Fox's. Now that your interview paper is finished, you'd better come home after school and get right to work."

"Oh, no," Leah begged, panic rising in her throat. "I can't give up visiting her. I'm the only friend she has. I help with the animals and she depends on me."

"I think your father is right, dear," Madeline Dvorak said softly. "You must concentrate on your studies."

Silence wrapped around Leah as she stared at the table's Formica top. What could she say to convince them that she needed Mrs. Fox and Mrs. Fox needed her?

Suddenly she jumped up. "Look," she said, pulling the list of words from her book. "She's given me books on pet care and explained these words." She thrust the vocabulary list at them.

Mr. Dvorak examined the list, nodding. "I'm pleased. But you also need to know history words."

"And science," Mrs. Dvorak said, her mouth stern but her eyes warm.

"I like science," Leah said earnestly. "We're starting a new unit on animals, and I've already got a headstart. Today in class I answered two questions. I know I'll do well on the test." She leaned forward eagerly. "The reading is easier, too. The reading is easier in all my subjects since Mrs. Fox has been helping me."

Her parents glanced at one another. Finally,

Mr. Dvorak said, "Then we'll wait for Miss Calvert's report. She said she'd send a note after the next test and let us know your progress. If your grades are still low, then we'll need to arrange a new study schedule."

Leah nodded. "I'll try," she promised gravely.

"You always say that," Mrs. Dvorak said with a resigned sigh, "but this time maybe you really mean it."

"It's bedtime, Pumpkin," her dad said, ruffling Leah's soft brown hair. He broke his sober expression with a smile.

As she slipped into her pajamas, she felt a little better. Still, why did she feel she was always making promises she couldn't keep? She yearned to please her parents, but by this time she knew she'd only let them down.

Snuggling beneath the covers, she looked over at her shelf of books. Beautiful books. A whole set of *World Myths and Legends*. She had leafed through the gift books that she'd received for birthdays and Christmases, and although she had glanced at the illustrations, she'd never read one legend. Some of the volumes were still in their cellophane wrappers. Mom and Dad had wanted to tempt her into reading by presenting her this gorgeous set of books. She stared at the thin books, all twenty of them. Blue, green, brown, red, with gold fancy lettering. "Rats!" she muttered, turning off the light and pummeling her pillow. Would she ever learn to love reading enough to satisfy her parents?

9

Witch's Assistant! Witch's Assistant!" Roseanne's words rang through her head. Why can't Roseanne and Danielle and the rest of them just leave me alone? Leah thought, as she doodled on a sheet of paper in the back booth of The Apple Tree. Her math book lay open before her, but she couldn't concentrate.

"Here, dear," her mother said, setting a cup of hot chocolate before her. "This is for being such a good studious girl."

Guiltily, she glanced up at her mother. If she only knew how little she'd accomplished since she'd come in. "How's Steven doing in the kitchen?" she asked, changing the subject.

"Very good. He's a great chef's assistant."

A twinge of jealousy shot through Leah. Steven was a chef's assistant, and she was a witch's assistant. It wasn't fair!

"Oh," Madeline Dvorak said, with a laugh, noticing Leah's downturned mouth, "Steven isn't perfect. He was a little on the hard side for the 'easy over' eggs, and he burned a pancake order, but other than that, he's been a big help."

Fine, Leah thought sourly. She knew what her parents thought of her help in the coffee shop. Not wanted. No more messed up checks were needed. Her face grew hot with humiliation at the memory of the disaster she'd created at the cash register. She pulled her math book toward her, but the figures blurred. Steven always did the right thing.

Mrs. Dvorak went into the kitchen as Steven came out. Her brother removed his long apron and tossed his white cap on the tabletop as he slid into the booth across from her. "Whew! What a morning!" He mopped his broad forehead and winked. "But I can use the experience. When I'm an archaeologist and out in the field, I may have to do my own cooking."

"I don't think you'll be frying eggs and mixing pancake batter in the Egyptian desert," Leah replied, closing her math book and sipping her hot chocolate.

"Maybe I will and maybe I won't," Steven said, "but at least I'll know how to fry lizard eggs."

"Ha, ha, ha," Leah retorted. "I know why you like this job. It's the money."

Steven gave a deep chuckle. "You're right! I've already saved $855 for college. Not bad, eh?"

She finished her hot chocolate, not replying. She wished she could save money. She could, too, if only she could work here. But why should Dad and Mom trust her? She'd not only lost money but customers as well, on that awful day!

"You're not at Mrs. Fox's today," Steven observed. "Did she finally throw you out?"

"No, she didn't. I'm going over there, but first I've got to do my homework," she said, tapping her pencil on her math book and screwing up her face. If there was one thing she hated it was homework.

Steven picked up her paper. "This doesn't look much like math homework to me."

She had forgotten about her drawing and hastily snatched the paper away from him.

"What kind of drawing was that? Looked like a bunch of boxes to me."

"I was rearranging the cages on Mrs. Fox's back porch. She needs more space and I'm drawing a better plan so she can have it. Yesterday she took in a ferret, a muskrat, and an opossum."

Steven threw back his head and let out a peal of laughter. "You may not be at Mrs. Fox's, Leah, but your mind is."

She blushed. "Guess it is," she mumbled. She

didn't expect Steven to understand.

"Danny McBride said she refused to take in a squirrel that had been hit by a car." Steven propped his elbows on the table and rested his square chin in his hands. "What do you think of your generous friend now?"

"That's because she's a pragmatist," Leah said.

"Whoa! Pragmatist! Listen to you! Bet you don't even know what the word means!"

"I do, too!" she said indignantly, folding the diagram of the cages and stuffing it in her jeans pocket. "Mrs. Fox calls herself a pragmatist. That's a person who sees things the way they really are — a practical person. She refuses to take in animals that have no hope 'cause she needs to save her time and energy for animals with a fighting chance."

Steven shrugged. "That makes sense," he said. "Danny lives in back of her. He said last year his mom called Mrs. Fox to complain about a crowing rooster that woke them up every morning at four-thirty. Mrs. Fox said she knew a farmer who'd take it off her hands, but if he didn't, she'd kill it and eat it."

Leah nodded in understanding. "Mrs. O'Neil next door called to ask Mrs. Fox to rescue a nest of duck eggs from her front yard, but Mrs. Fox said not to worry about them. If the eggs hatched, she'd come and take the ducklings, but chances were that the raccoons would eat them."

"Now I know why you like her," Steven said with a grin. "She's weird — like you."

Leah bristled. More and more she found herself defending Mrs. Fox. "She isn't weird."

"Enjoy these," Madeline Dvorak said, setting a plate of kolaches in front of them. "Your father just made them."

"Prune filling?" Steven said with a quizzical glance, reaching for one of the sweet-filled buns.

"Poppyseed," she answered, watching them each take a pastry.

Leah bit into the poppyseed-stuffed dessert. She loved these warm sweets and so did the customers. They flocked to the coffee shop every Saturday noon for this fresh-baked treat.

"Did you finish your homework, Leah?" her mother asked.

"Hmmmm, almost," she responded noncommittally. "I promised Mrs. Fox I'd be over by noon."

"When you've finished your math, you can go," Mrs. Dvorak said, her blue-gray eyes warm yet serious. She gently smoothed down Leah's shirt collar.

Wearily, Leah reached for her book. The problems were so long and complicated it would take her forever to finish! She stared at her math book, not wanting to show her mother that she'd only figured out one compound interest problem.

"Your father will be back to check on your progress." She gave Leah's shoulder a squeeze, then turned and left.

Steven grinned at Leah. "Want some help?"

Ordinarily she would reject his offer, but today she welcomed it. She wanted to get going. She shoved her book at him, and he diligently worked through all the problems.

After thirty minutes Jan Dvorak reviewed the work and smiled, patting her head. "Good work, Leah. You can leave for Mrs. Fox's."

"Thanks," she said, her face clouding with uneasiness. She hated to deceive her dad.

"I know you've been waiting for my OK," he said in sudden good humor, wiping his hands on an apron that puffed out over his round stomach. "You're like a runner at the starting line." He shook his head at her eagerness. "I'm glad you and Mrs. Fox get along so well, Pumpkin. Just keep up your schoolwork." His stubby fingers touched her cheek. "You're so pretty — look just like your mother."

"But I'm not as smart," she murmured.

"Nonsense, you're as smart as anyone else. I'm not worried. Someday," he cast his eyes on Steven and grinned, "you'll pass up your big brother."

"Ha!" Steven said, a mocking smile spreading over his wide face. "That'll be the day!"

Leah glanced at her brother. That *would* be the day. And a day that would never happen. But she was pleased that her dad believed in her. She was also pleased that Steven hadn't told Dad he'd done most of her homework.

"Have you baked all the kolaches?" she asked.

"Yes," her father said, and when the bell jingled above the door, he adjusted his white cap. "And here comes part of the noon crowd to gobble them up. Time to go to work. See you two later at home." Placing a flour-smudged finger on Leah's nose, he added, "And don't overdo the work at Mrs. Fox's, Leah. Your mom might want some help at home, too."

"I won't," she replied with a smile, jumping up and hugging her dad. "See you soon."

Whistling, she went on her way, carrying a bag of goodies for Mrs. Fox. Mom had fixed a ham sandwich and put in four kolaches. Her parents didn't disapprove of Blanche Fox, yet they were too busy to visit her with Leah. If Leah could only get them interested in going over there, she was sure other neighbors on Tall Trees Lane would follow.

Going up the walk to Mrs. Fox's, she patted

the brass deer that guarded the porch. Where's Flora? she wondered, looking around for the real deer. But Flora wasn't in sight.

Inside, Leah hung up her jeans jacket. Mrs. Fox greeted her, then went on feeding two baby squirrels with an eyedropper. "Matilda's better," she said, not wasting any words.

"Really?" Leah rushed over to the gray cat, who was sitting up and grooming herself.

"Matilda! You look wonderful. If only you weren't so skinny." She closely examined the cat, who began to purr at her gentle touch. "Your eyes are brighter, and you've cleaned your plate. Good girl!"

"A couple more weeks and we'll find a nice home for her," Mrs. Fox said, rising and placing the tiny squirrels in a cage.

While Ozzie bounced around her, Leah refilled Matilda's water bowl, then the plate of dried food. Ozzie leaped up and licked Leah's cheek, but Matilda, already accustomed to the household, ignored the rambunctious pup.

"Come over to the McBrides' with me," Mrs. Fox said, rising and covering the baby squirrels with a piece of flannel. "Mrs. McBride's called twice. Flora is loose and munching on their front yard. Mrs. McBride is having a fit."

At the McBrides', Flora, her four spindly legs firmly planted, was gazing placidly at two animal control officers.

Mrs. McBride, a tall raw-boned woman with big beefy arms, poked her head out the front door. "Get that wretched deer off my yard!" she shouted to the officers.

The taller of the two smiled, spotting Leah and Mrs. Fox approaching. "We'll let Mrs. Fox do that. How ya doin', Mrs. Fox?"

Mrs. McBride's cheeks reddened angrily. "If you two did your job," she complained, jabbing her finger in the air, "you'd do the work yourself!" She took a long breath. "You treat Mrs. Fox better than anyone else! Don't her neighbors have any rights? After all, we're the ones being disturbed!"

Embarrassed, Leah gave Mrs. Fox a sidelong glance, but Mrs. Fox didn't seem to mind Mrs. McBride's words. Well, Leah thought, obviously Mrs. Fox was used to her neighbor's criticism, but *she* wasn't. It was all she could do to keep from shouting back at Mrs. McBride.

"Mrs. Fox is helping the environment," the young man explained, his bearded face calm. "We need her, Mrs. McBride."

"Maybe you should nominate her for sainthood!" Mrs. McBride huffed.

The young man grinned at Mrs. Fox. "Maybe we should."

At that Mrs. McBride turned around and went inside, slamming the door behind her.

Mrs. Fox chuckled grimly. "John, you're my only cheerleader. You and Margaret." She nodded pleasantly to the officer next to him.

John rubbed his stubby beard, his face sobering. "We got a problem here, Mrs. Fox. Can you get your doe back to your place?"

"Sure can," she answered confidently, strolling up to Flora and wrapping her arm around the deer's neck. "Come on, girl, we're going home." Soon she had the deer moving meekly along with her.

"Thanks!" Margaret called. "Is it OK if we bring over a woodchuck we found downtown on a window ledge? It seems to be in shock."

"Bring him over," Mrs. Fox said, waving her hand in acknowledgment. As she walked beside Flora, her shirttail flapping in the breeze, she leaned over and spoke softly in the deer's ear.

Leah trailed behind, marveling at the touch that Mrs. Fox had with animals. If only Mrs. Fox had that touch with people, Leah thought for the umpteenth time, she'd never be lonesome.

10

Leah eagerly waited for the reports to be returned. It was almost time for the bell and Miss Calvert was explaining the use of *lie* and *lay*. Why didn't she hand the papers back? The stacked reports were so inviting that she was ready to jump out of her seat, dash up, and thumb through them to find her grade.

"So for tomorrow's homework," Miss Calvert said, "write out the exercises on page 53." She glanced at the clock. "Now I want to hand back your interviews. I enjoyed reading them very much." Her dark eyes shone as she surveyed the class. Then she moved down the aisles, passing out the papers.

Leah glanced back at Roseanne who met her eyes, then hopefully held up two crossed fingers. Leah smiled. Roseanne was friendly, but things hadn't been the same since Leah had been spending so much time at Mrs. Fox's. Clearly Roseanne resented the fact that Leah was never available.

"Leah," Miss Calvert said, handing her her paper, "this was very well done. I'd like to talk to you about it."

Leah's breath caught in her throat when she glimpsed the big red A at the top! Her first A! She smiled up at Miss Calvert, indicating she'd be glad to see her anytime. This would be one talk she wouldn't mind. Her heart beat wildly, and she could hardly sit still as she studied Miss Calvert's comments:

You need a period here.
You ignore commas. Study page 46 in your
grammar book.

But her last remark was the best.

Excellent, Leah. This paper is the best you've done!
If you apply yourself, you can do A work.

She turned to face Roseanne. "What'd you get?" she mouthed.

Roseanne made a tepee of her fingers and smiled. She should have guessed that Roseanne would get an A, too, but it didn't matter. She nodded happily, a wide smile creasing her face.

"Me, too," she whispered proudly.

When the bell rang, she fell in step beside Roseanne. "Let's go to the mall and celebrate our A's," she said. "It's my first one." She didn't mind confessing to Roseanne. Her best friend knew how difficult school was for her.

Roseanne's blue eyes widened. "You mean you're not going over to Mrs. Fox's?"

"Only to feed Matilda."

"Matilda?"

Leah laughed. "Matilda's a stray cat I'm nursing back to health. I need to check on her progress." She'd forgotten how long it had been since she'd seen Roseanne. She didn't even know about all of Mrs. Fox's wonderful animals. She gave Roseanne a warm look. "I can meet you at Sandy's Cafe at four-thirty," Leah said with a smile, fairly skipping along.

"Four-thirty it is." Roseanne's return smile was just as warm. "It's been forever since we've hung out together."

"Too long," Leah murmured. Silently she promised to make it up to Roseanne by finding more time to be with her. Next week she'd invite her to spend the night.

Roseanne giggled. "I've got a million things to tell you."

"Me, too," Leah answered lightly, going into

her science class with a bouncy step.

The day went fast. She sat through science in a state of excitement, every once in a while pulling out her English paper to gaze at the A. What would Mom and Dad say when she showed them her paper? For once they'd be proud of her. She reread Miss Calvert's comments on the bottom again, mulling them over. Could she really do A work? No way! She shoved the paper back into her folder. An A wouldn't happen again in a hundred years. But maybe, if she "applied" herself as her teachers and counselors had been urging her to do, she could pull it off. She shifted her thoughts to concentrate on what Mr. Gonser was saying.

Leah was soon caught up in his lecture about wildlife. She already knew that you shouldn't take in wild animals as pets unless you knew they were orphaned or needed care. Leah knew Mrs. Fox handled only animals that needed her attention, and when they were well, she knew just how to release them. She never set them free where there was too much traffic or commotion. And Mrs. Fox had the cooperation of the Animal Control Agency, which brought her injured animals and sometimes took the healed animals out to the forest preserve. She smiled when she remembered how furious Mrs. McBride had been when the agency officers had said that if they could they'd nominate Mrs. Fox for sainthood.

When the bell rang, she was still thinking of Mrs. Fox. Why couldn't neighbors like Mrs. McBride appreciate Mrs. Fox? If there were only some way she could bring them together!

Putting her books in her locker she hurried out the door, planning her agenda. She'd make a quick stop at Mrs. Fox's, then hurry on to the mall to meet Roseanne. After they had a Coke, maybe they'd have time to go to Renée's Dress Shoppe. She'd show Roseanne a fringed-leather vest she'd been wanting for a long time.

Hurrying along, she breathed in the fall air, thinking how perfect the day was. The drifting red and orange leaves and the tang in the air meant winter was just around the corner. But first things first. Next week was Halloween. She'd celebrate with her friends. Maybe she'd rent a spooky movie and have Terry, Mike, Danielle, and Roseanne over. Mom and Dad would let her do almost anything when they saw her grade! She picked up her pace, not wanting to be late in meeting Roseanne. Feeding Matilda wouldn't take long.

Ringing the doorbell, she waited impatiently for an answer. When Mrs. Fox didn't come, she went to the brass deer on the lawn and tipped it forward, taking the key from under his foreleg and unlocking the door. Where was Mrs. Fox? she wondered. Going to Matilda's corner, Leah was pleased by how shiny the cat's fur had become and how her ribs were filling out.

Mrs. Fox rushed in from the back. "Leah!" she said. "I'm glad you're here. I went out to the garage to get a basket. Thought I might have to take Sara and Gus to the vet."

"What's wrong with the baby squirrels?" Leah asked. "They're all right, aren't they?"

"They will be. I hope." Mrs. Fox said, going to the opened bird cage where the two tiny red squirrels sprawled unmoving. "They won't eat or take water," she said, gently rubbing Gus's head. "Dr. Vanoff said it wasn't necessary to bring them to his office. Wild animals raised by humans often lack certain vitamins because they were deprived too early of their mother's milk." She fished in her pocket and handed Leah a prescription. "Would you be a dear and run to the drug store for this medicine?"

"Right away," Leah answered, rushing out. She took the porch steps two at a time. She hoped the red squirrels would be all right. Mrs. Fox had spent so much time with them, and they had been getting along so well! Then all of a sudden the lively babies had become weak and sickly.

It wasn't until she was at the drug store and waiting for the prescription that her heart jumped. Roseanne! She glanced at her watch — four-twenty. Oh, no, she thought, momentary panic sweeping through her. She'd be late. She must hurry. Grabbing the prescription, she raced out and down the sidewalk. But her heart quieted as she neared Mrs. Fox's. Certainly Roseanne would wait for her. She'd drop off the medicine, explain that she couldn't stay and go directly to the mall.

But when she got back, Mrs. Fox asked her to feed Ozzie, for she had her hands full in feeding the squirrels their medicine with an eyedropper. Also Flora and Mr. McTavish had to be fed and several other animals. Leah couldn't refuse when Mrs. Fox needed her help. With fingers that trembled in her haste, she filled Ozzie's bowl and replenished Mr. McTavish's birdseed. She was pleased that the bright green parrot no longer told her to go away. When she had finished feeding the animals, she called out, "I've got to meet Roseanne, Mrs. Fox, but I'll be back tomorrow."

Mrs. Fox didn't look up when Leah went flying out the door.

When she arrived at Sandy's Cafe, she peered down the row of booths, but Roseanne wasn't there. She walked outside and looked up and down the street, but no Roseanne. Going back in, she asked the waitress if a pretty blonde girl had been there.

"About your age?" she asked, shifting her tray to her other hip.

"Yes," Leah answered breathlessly.

"She left about thirty minutes ago," she said, brushing past Leah.

Oh, no, Leah thought, a heavy feeling growing in her stomach. No wonder Roseanne had left. It was already five-thirty. Miserably, she turned toward home. Roseanne would never understand why she'd been stood up. She'd be furious! Suddenly, she felt a burning behind her eyes. She was scared. Scared that she'd lost her best friend.

11

The next day Leah rushed to Roseanne's locker so she could apologize. But when Roseanne caught sight of her, she abruptly turned away.

"Roseanne," she said, "I'm sorry I couldn't make it yesterday, but Mrs. Fox had an emergency, and — "

"What kind of an emergency?" she snapped, confronting her with a skeptical look on her face.

"Two baby squirrels were sick and — "

Roseanne interrupted. "Two sick squirrels? Now I've heard everything. You're just full of excuses, aren't you, Leah? For your information I waited at Sandy's Cafe for over half an hour!"

"I'm sorry," Leah repeated. "It couldn't be helped. Mrs. Fox needed me."

Roseanne stuck a hand on her hip. "I'm not waiting for you anymore!" Her voice trembled, and she lifted her small chin. "Mrs. Fox is your friend — your *only* friend! From now on, stick with her, 'cause you sure won't have me! I'm sorry I wasted my time on you!"

Leah flung out her hands in a helpless gesture. "Please, Roseanne. I'll make it up to you." A tremulous smile flitted over her lips. "I'll buy you a Coke after school," she offered shyly.

"No, thanks!" Roseanne said haughtily. "I'm going over to Danielle's."

With hot tears stinging her eyes, Leah stood forlornly in the hall, watching Roseanne stalk away. She didn't know what to do. She'd lost her best friend, and the students hurrying by didn't even care. She turned toward the classroom, but how she dreaded sitting through English! She and Roseanne had had so many good times together. The memory of the day she'd worn her mother's locket and lost it flooded over her. She and Roseanne had been at a Fourth of July band concert when Leah had discovered the locket was missing. Roseanne had stayed long after the concert to help her search. They had hunted in the stands and over the grounds. It was almost dark when Roseanne triumphantly held up the golden necklace. How happy they had been, laughing and dancing and singing across the empty bandstand. Now those good times had ended.

When the halls were almost clear, Leah resignedly entered Miss Calvert's room. Walking by

Roseanne, she didn't dare look at her. Yet she yearned to stop at her desk and say something friendly to her. She slipped into her seat, feeling a burning sensation creep along her spine and up the base of her neck. She was certain Roseanne's glaring eyes were fastened on her. Leah wondered if Danielle knew about their fight? Or Terry? Or Mike? If they didn't know, they soon would. Roseanne would never forgive her. She was so angry that she'd make certain her friends wouldn't associate with Leah, either.

Leah wasn't sure how she got through the class, but at last the bell rang. She didn't attempt to catch up with Roseanne and Danielle, for they were obviously talking about her. Once Danielle glanced over her shoulder and gave her a hateful look. Leah wished she could crawl into a hole and disappear like a hibernating winter bear. Maybe by spring Roseanne would talk to her again. But spring was a long way off.

All day she felt awful, but when she arrived at Mrs. Fox's, the animals cheered her up. Gus and Sara gazed at her with bright eyes, and although the baby squirrels weren't their usual frisky selves, they clearly were feeling better. After chatting with the two cats, Willie and Sima, she set to work. She scrubbed cages as if her life depended on their cleanliness, then fed Mr. McTavish and

Jack, the raccoon. With her mind so occupied, some of her misery gradually evaporated.

Later Mrs. Fox entered from the back porch with Ozzie romping at her heels. She wore hip boots, jeans, and a heavy plaid jacket. "Let's stop, Leah," she said, removing her felt-brimmed hat and hanging it on the wall hook. "You've worked like a trooper for two hours, and it's time for a breather. I'll brew some jasmine tea."

Sitting across from Mrs. Fox at the kitchen table, Leah wrapped her hands around the steaming mug. She was tired. The thought of losing Roseanne filled her with despair. She tried to hide her hurt, but it was no use. Mrs. Fox knew her too well.

"What's wrong, Leah?" Mrs. Fox asked quietly.

Leah studied her tea, swirling the heavily scented liquid around, but she soon found herself pouring out the whole story of Roseanne's rejection. She ended by saying, "So Roseanne won't have anything to do with me." Her voice cracked. "She was my best friend, too."

For a moment all Leah could hear was Ozzie's contented snuffles as he slept at the feet of Mrs. Fox. At last Mrs. Fox said, "It seems I'm messing up your life, too." A sad smile twitched at the corners of her mouth. "I'm not worth losing your friends over, Leah. I think it's time you stopped coming here. Stay away from me and you'll soon win your friends back." Absentmindedly she reached down and scratched behind Ozzie's floppy ears. The pup whimpered softly in his dreams.

Leah wondered if the spaniel was dreaming of chasing Matilda, the cat. As if reading her thoughts, Matilda brushed against her leg. "Are you hungry?" she questioned the cat, bending down and running her hand over Matilda's sleek fur. She didn't want Mrs. Fox to see her sudden tears. "Mrs. Fox, I feel as if this is my second home," she choked. "I could never stop coming to see you."

Mrs. Fox rounded the table and silently stood in back of Leah's chair. She rested her hands on Leah's shoulders and placed her leathery cheek next to hers. "I must confess I'd miss you if you left, dear." Hastily she picked up the two mugs, and took them to the sink. "It's good to have a friend like you. I didn't realize how much I needed you until just now, when I suggested you stop coming." Her voice was hoarse, and she kept her back turned.

Leah tried to swallow, but the lump in her throat prevented it. Mrs. Fox was a quiet person who didn't often demonstrate affection. But today she had been different. Mrs. Fox had a warm heart and was a wonderful friend. Maybe Leah had lost Roseanne, but she and Mrs. Fox had become even closer.

Their companionable silence was shattered by a knock on the back door.

Mrs. Fox blew her nose, then opened the door. Her eyebrows raised a notch, but that was the only evidence of surprise she gave when she confronted the cantankerous Mrs. McBride. "Well?" she asked. "What is it?"

Mrs. McBride, who towered over Mrs. Fox, opened her coat, revealing a small frightened blue jay cradled in her hand. "I found this critter flopping around on my front lawn. Something's wrong with its wing."

Leah peered over Mrs. Fox's shoulder. The blue jay's wing drooped forlornly.

"I think its wing is broken," Mrs. McBride said, her eyes fearfully scanning Mrs. Fox's face. "I wondered if you'd take it in."

"I don't know," Mrs. Fox said doubtfully. "I'm filled up. Did you call the agency?"

"No," Mrs. McBride admitted. "I just saw the poor thing and knew it needed help. You were the nearest so I brought him right over."

"I suppose I have room for one more bird." Gently Mrs. Fox took the blue jay and examined the wing. "Hmmm," she said, "I'll tape the wing close to its body, and it will be as good as new."

"After the ruckus I created over your deer," Mrs. McBride said, eyes narrowing beneath heavy gray brows, "I wouldn't blame you if you slammed the door in my face."

"I'd never do that." Blanche Fox's dark eyes shone. "Especially if you brought me a hurt bird."

"Well," Mrs. McBride said abruptly. "I see it's in good hands." She half turned, then added hesitantly, "And thanks." She pulled her coat closer about her, and hurried away.

When Leah saw it was six o'clock, she grabbed her sweater, exclaiming, "I've got to go, Mrs. Fox. This is the second time this week I've been late for supper. Mom's gonna kill me."

"You run along, Leah. I've mended a hundred broken wings." She gave Leah a side glance. "Will I see you tomorrow?"

"Of course," Leah said promptly. "And I'll bring you some more kolaches. I know how much you like them." She slipped into her sweater. "Gotta rush. 'Bye."

Going out the door and down the steps, she smiled when she remembered how Mrs. McBride's voice had changed from a grating tone to a softer, gentler one. When Mrs. McBride needed help, she knew whom to turn to. And if Mrs. Fox could win over Mrs. McBride there was no reason she couldn't win over the rest of the neighborhood.

12

Leah's mouth felt like sandpaper, dry and scratchy, as she dismally pushed open the door. School was out, and she was going home for the day. The crisp afternoon air, however, didn't buoy her sunken spirits. She'd almost failed a math test and it was going to be a lonely Halloween. She had no plans. Not one. Steven was going to a party, and all she had to look forward to was staying home with her mom and dad. Her mom planned to make caramel corn while Leah answered the doorbell. She'd "ooh" and "ahhh" over all the little kids' costumes, then go to bed.

That would be her exciting, scary Halloween. Before, she'd always been with her friends, but now they hated her. A flash of loneliness stabbed through her. Roseanne and Danielle had deserted her.

Bleakly, she remembered when she'd received her first A. Was that only a few days ago? How happy she'd been. She'd planned to rent a spooky movie and have the gang over. Since Roseanne and Danielle weren't speaking to her, though, she had no one to ask. She missed her close girlfriends. The three of them had a special bond.

She turned at the sound of voices. Terry and Mike hurled themselves toward her. Big Mike teasingly shoved Terry against her shoulder. "He likes you," Mike said, letting out a big guffaw.

Leah sighed. Boys were so immature. They were always shoving, pulling, or pushing one another. She walked faster, trying to ignore them. Secretly though, she was pleased. At least *they* didn't shun her.

"Terry likes you," Mike repeated, rubbing his hands in glee. "Even if you are a witch's assistant."

Pressing together her lips, she bit back a sharp retort. She looked straight ahead and kept walking. And she'd been thinking nice things about them, too!

"Can't you talk?" Terry teased. His red jacket was unzipped, flopping loosely in the wind. "Hey, witch's assistant, are you going over to Mrs. Fox's to brew up a magic potion?" He stuck his hands into his pockets, his black eyes glittering mischievously.

And Terry was supposed to like her, she

thought, frowning at him. The rat! He was like all the rest! "For your information, Terry O'Bannion," she said, "I'm going home."

"Hey, Leah, where's Danielle and Roseanne?" Mike asked, a puzzled expression on his face.

She shrugged, pretending not to care. "How should I know?"

"Didn't Roseanne tell you?" Terry said. "She and Leah had a big fight. Roseanne thinks Leah's spending too much time with the Witch of Tall Trees Lane and doesn't need her friends anymore."

"Don't — call — Mrs. Fox — a witch," Leah said emphatically.

"Oh, pardon me," Terry singsonged, dancing around her. "I forgot. She's just a sweet little old lady."

"And she's not *old*, either," Leah said sharply.

"OK, OK," Terry said, throwing up his hands in mock surrender. "Whatever you say."

Leah gave him a side glance, and she knew he was sorry. She couldn't stop a smile from spreading across her face.

Terry grinned, showing even white teeth. She felt warm and friendly toward him again.

"Tonight," Mike said cheerfully, "we're going to have fun! We might even pay the witch a visit. . . ." He stopped when he saw Leah's glare,

"I mean *Mrs. Fox*. It's Halloween, and who knows what might happen," he added mysteriously.

A tingle of apprehension skipped along her spine. "What do you mean?"

"Nothing. *Nothing*," Mike said quickly. "Forget it. C'mon, Terry."

She watched as they sauntered away, whistling innocently. She knew they were plotting something. Well, if she knew Terry and Mike, they'd be too afraid to trespass on the "witch's" land. She shouldn't worry. But she did anyway. It was Halloween, and they might try anything.

That night Leah huddled in the large wingback chair before the fireplace. A few little kids knocked on the door and she offered them candy, but it wasn't much fun, and she hardly noticed their costumes and painted faces. She went to bed early, certain she wouldn't sleep.

But she soon drifted off. Dreams flitted in and out of her subconscious, but the most horrifying one was a ghost that chased her, floating above her. It hovered near, beckoning, and in a deep voice intoned, "Come with me, witch's assistant. I need you."

Frightened, Leah backed away, but the ghost pursued her. Laughing fiendishly, the ghost moved forward, then retreated. In her terror Leah clutched at the sheet. To her astonishment, the sheet came off in her hand and there stood Roseanne. But it was a Roseanne she'd never seen before. Wild hair encircled her head like a silver bramble bush, and her eyes glowed brighter than sapphires. Menacingly, she curled her hands over her head, her long crimson fingernails waving to and fro.

Roseanne glided closer. Leah gasped, panting for air. She tried to escape but stumbled and fell. Roseanne's sharp nails clawed her arm. "Witch's Assistant!" she howled.

"Ooooh," Leah groaned in alarm, sitting bolt upright in bed and attempting to shake the fearful image from her mind. Her heart thundered in her ears, and her pajamas stuck to her clammy skin. For a long time she stared into the blackness. Did Roseanne hate her that much? Tomorrow Leah would go to Roseanne's house and try to make up with her. She had to try. She didn't want to be without Roseanne any longer.

Eventually Leah closed her eyes, but she didn't sleep for a long time.

Saturday morning she awoke feeling as if a train had rumbled over her. But after washing her face she felt better. She'd visit Mrs. Fox first, then go over to Roseanne's. Things would be all right, she thought, pulling on her heavy sweater. She knew they would.

But when she arrived at Mrs. Fox's, she was shocked by what she saw. Toilet tissue was woven in and out through the treetops and around every branch. The bushes were covered, too, and the paper curled around the porch and up to the roof. The brass deer was missing from its place on the lawn and had been hauled to the top of the roof. Ropes dangled down the side of the house. Upset cages dotted the ground, and red paint was splattered across the front of the house. In large letters was scrawled, *The Witch of Tall Trees Lane.*

Leah shook her head, her throat so tight she couldn't swallow. Who could have done such an awful thing? Halloween or no Halloween, there was no excuse for this! A panic-stricken thought struck her. Mrs. Fox! Was she all right?

Breathless, she burst into the house. "Mrs. Fox!" she yelled. "Mrs. Fox!" Where was she? She rushed through the living room and into the dining room.

"I'm in here," came a dull voice.

She dashed into the kitchen. Mrs. Fox, her head bowed and her body slumped in despair, sat at the table.

"Oh, Mrs. Fox. How awful! What happened?" she gasped.

Mrs. Fox glanced at her with mournful eyes. "I don't know why they did this. No one's ever bothered me before. Why would they do this?"

"Oh, I'm so sorry," Leah said, putting her arm around Mrs. Fox's shoulder. "I'll help you clean up."

Mrs. Fox stared at her with pain-glazed eyes. "The worst thing is Ozzie."

Leah's stomach clenched tight. "Ozzie?" she asked, afraid of what she might hear.

"He's gone." The color had drained from Mrs. Fox's face, and it was obvious she hadn't slept the night before.

"Gone?" Leah echoed numbly.

"I had put him outside on a rope and someone unfastened him. He's lost. He'll never find his way back. He's only a puppy."

"Oh, Mrs. Fox," Leah whispered, sinking into a chair. "Why didn't you call me?"

"I was out most of the night hunting for Ozzie. I knew you'd be over this morning."

"I'll put up notices," Leah said positively. "Someone will find Ozzie." She placed a hand over Mrs. Fox's calloused ones. "Don't worry. We'll find him." But she was scared Ozzie was lost for good. "Did you see who did this?"

"After I returned from searching the neighborhood, I saw a group of kids running down the street. They wore masks and were about your size." She rose and stared out the window. Her usual lively expression had been replaced by a look of defeat.

Leah's blood ran cold. *Kids her size* did this? Could her friends have done such a thing? No. It was impossible! They weren't that cruel.

But then she remembered Mike's words, "We might even pay the witch a visit. . . ."

13

I'm going home to change into old clothes, Mrs. Fox," Leah said. "Then I'll be back to help clean up this mess." She looked out the window at the empty overturned cages. She was grateful there hadn't been any animals in them.

"Don't hurry," Mrs. Fox answered, moving to the bedroom. "Since I didn't sleep last night, I'm going to take a rest. Run along, dear." Wearily she turned away and Leah's heart went out to her. Why did bad things have to happen to such nice people?

All the way home, Leah wondered if her friends were the ones who had made a disaster area of Mrs. Fox's yard. If they had, she didn't want anything more to do with them. And to think she'd been on her way over to Roseanne's to make up with her!

Well, she thought sourly, forget it. On the other hand, maybe she was jumping to conclusions.

Maybe the gang hadn't done anything. Maybe high school kids had turned Mrs. Fox's yard upside down. But as she approached her house, she knew better. Hadn't Mrs. Fox said the kids were about her height? High school kids would have been taller.

With determined steps she turned in the opposite direction. Her friends were probably at the mall, and she'd find out once and for all who was responsible.

When she went into Sandy's Cafe, she immediately glimpsed Roseanne's blonde head in the back booth. She was talking and laughing with Danielle, Mike, and Terry.

Without thinking she went directly up to their booth and blurted out, "Were you guys at Mrs. Fox's last night?"

"Sure were," Mike chortled, not trying to hide anything. "We really outfoxed the fox lady, didn't we?"

"Why?" Danielle questioned, smiling innocently. "Have you been over there?"

"Yes, I have," she said. Her heart plummeted to her shoes. So they *were* the ones! Her eyes flashed, and she put her hands on her hips. "Did you let Ozzie loose?" she asked, glaring from one to the other.

"Ozzie?" Mike shrugged. "Who's Ozzie?"

"Ozzie's a puppy, who's just about Mrs. Fox's only friend. And now he's missing. What has Mrs. Fox done to you that you could be so mean?"

"Hey," Terry said with a grin, "lighten up, Leah. The paint's washable, and we only played a few pranks. What's the big deal? Isn't that what Halloween is all about?"

She ignored his question, asking another. "And how's Mrs. Fox supposed to get that heavy brass deer off the roof?"

"I'm sure you'll think of something," Roseanne said in a silky voice. "You're over there all the time! Between the two of you, you'll figure it out."

"I think you're all hateful," Leah said, her eyes stinging with hot tears. "You should come back to Mrs. Fox's and help me straighten things out. That's the least you can do."

"No way," Danielle said. "We're going to the movies."

"Come with me," Leah repeated. "You can help look for Ozzie. After all," she said, a faint tremor in her voice, "you're the ones that turned him loose."

For a short period her four friends were silent. Mike bent his head, slurping up the last of his Coke. Roseanne and Danielle met each other's eyes, exchanging solemn looks.

Glancing sheepishly at Leah, Terry said in a

low hesitant tone, "The dog will turn up. He's probably there right now."

"He's only a puppy," Leah said in a tight voice. "So after the mess you've made, you're just going to walk away and go to the movies! Well, I hope you choke on your popcorn!"

Once she was out of the cafe, she raced past the shoppers and stores, tears blurring her eyes. Her friends were vicious and mean! How could she ever have liked them? She knew Roseanne had been part of the vandalism because she was mad at Leah. And all Leah had done was miss a date for a Coke! She'd tried to explain, but Roseanne wouldn't listen. Roseanne was jealous, Leah thought with irritation, just plain jealous that Leah had another friend.

Leah lifted her chin and let the tears roll down her cheeks, not caring what people thought. Well, if that was the way Roseanne wanted to be, she'd have no more to do with her! She was glad she'd found her out in time! Never in a thousand years would she beg her forgiveness! Never, never, never!

"Hey, watch where you're going!" a young boy warned after she'd bumped into him.

A sob tore at her throat, and she dashed outdoors, away from the mall and down the sidewalk. She was glad to be alone at last. Who needed

Roseanne? Or Danielle? Or Mike? Or Terry? She had plenty to do without them. She wondered if Steven would help but remembered that her brother was working at the coffee shop today. So were Mom and Dad. Any yard cleaning would be up to her.

After going home to change, Leah returned to Mrs. Fox's. Angrily she rolled up her sleeves. First, she attacked the bushes near the house, tearing off the toilet tissue, balling it into a wad, and throwing it on the ground. She continued to pull off sheets and sheets of paper until every bush was clean.

She had almost cleared the paper-strewn trees when Mrs. Fox came out with several large plastic bags. She appeared to feel a bit better having slept, and when she looked around, a smile stretched slowly across her small dark face. "Leah, bless your heart," she said softly. "You've worked wonders. The place looks better already." The weariness was gone from Mrs. Fox's voice, the tired and haggard lines had disappeared from her face. Leah stared at Mrs. Fox in amazement, marveling at her grit and stamina. She certainly didn't let anything get her down for long.

For several hours they worked side by side, ridding the yard of all debris. Next they tackled the cages and set them upright in a neat row.

After washing off the splatters of red paint, they began on the hateful phrase, *Witch of Tall Trees Lane*. Leah glanced worriedly at Mrs. Fox, but she was silent as she grimly scrubbed off one word after the other.

When they were finished, Leah stood back admiring the house. It actually looked better than it ever had. The raked leaves and scattered debris beneath the bushes had been piled high, leaving the yard neat and clean. She was proud of how much she'd accomplished. And even though Mrs. Fox didn't say anything, she knew she was pleased, too.

Leah squinted up at the slanted roof. "Now for the deer," she said with determination. "Is there a way up there?"

Blanche Fox nodded. "There's an outside stairway on the balcony, but I'll go up with you."

"I can handle it," Leah said confidently, surveying the deer that stood beside the brick chimney. Her back and arms ached, but she was determined to finish before dark. The blue sky had dark purple streaks, and dusk had fallen. She knew, though, that she could finish one more task. Hurriedly, she went inside and up the stairs.

Climbing out onto the balcony, she clambered up the ladder stairs and onto the roof. She bent down and lifted up the ropes that swung loosely down the side of the house. Tying the rope around the deer's belly, she braced herself to haul the statue forward. She was glad she was wearing sneakers so she could gain a foothold. The brass deer was heavy, and she strained every muscle to drag it across the roof toward the edge in order to lower it.

"Are you all right, Leah?" Mrs. Fox called, waiting below.

Leah peered down over the eaves. From this height Mrs. Fox's features were almost indistinct.

"I'm fine," she said, panting and straining at the ropes. Finally, she had almost gotten the deer to the roof's rim but wondered if she could hold it once it was pushed over the side. She would need every ounce of strength to lower it.

"I'm coming up to help you," Mrs. Fox said firmly. "Don't let go until I'm up there."

Leah didn't argue. It would require both of them to get it down safely. She got behind the deer, shoving it a little closer to the edge. A movement caught her eye, and she glanced below. There stood Roseanne gazing up at her. For a moment their eyes locked. Leah didn't dare breathe. Why didn't Roseanne move on? What was she waiting for? She was probably gloating over the trouble she and the others had caused.

"OK, Leah, let's lower the deer," said Mrs. Fox,

creeping carefully around the chimney stack. Leah continued to stare at Roseanne. At last, Roseanne bent her head and hurried on. Leah turned to secure the ropes. Maybe, she thought, Roseanne had felt a twinge of guilt. If she had, she certainly hadn't showed it. Bracing her feet, Leah tugged on the rope, moving the deer halfway over the edge. She tried to forget about Roseanne. But the image of her unblinking stare was imprinted on her mind.

14

On Monday morning when Leah got out of bed, every muscle screamed in protest. Moving like a robot, stiff and aching, she peered at herself in the bathroom mirror. It looked as if she'd been in a cat fight. A jagged scratch, from a toilet papered tree branch, zigzagged down her cheek, and her hands were sore and raw from rope burns. Lowering the brass deer hadn't been easy, but she and Mrs. Fox had managed to set it down without any harm.

Today she longed to stay home from school but knew better than to even ask. Not only did she want to play hooky because her body ached, but because she hated to face her friends after everything that had happened.

When she came down for breakfast, Steven glanced up from his book. "Hi. I saved you a banana for your cereal."

"Thanks," she murmured, shaking bran flakes

into a bowl and peeling the banana. Steven was all right for a big brother. Yesterday he'd helped bag leaves from Mrs. Fox's yard, repaired two window shutters, and trimmed the hedges.

"I'm glad you helped Mrs. Fox," she said gratefully, pouring a glass of milk. "We could never have finished without you."

"No problem," he said, rising and grabbing his book. He paused, "But I'll expect a big favor from you one of these days."

"You've got it," she said.

"Mrs. Fox sure appreciated all I did for her," Steven said. "You know, she's pretty neat."

"Haven't I been telling you that?" Leah said with a grin.

"She's younger than I thought, too."

"Haven't I been telling you that?" she repeated.

Steven laughed. "Guess you know her better than anyone else." He took a final swallow of milk. "And that parrot is something else again," he said. "Mr. McTavish is my favorite."

"Even though he told you to 'go away'?" she said with a laugh. "You know, Steven, Mrs. Fox has a lot of wonderful animals. I like Matilda, the gray cat, but we're having trouble giving her away. No one wants an old cat."

"Someone will take her."

"Fat chance," she said. "No one wants to have

anything to do with Mrs. Fox, or her animals."

"Can't you think of some way to get the neighbors over there?" He grinned and his round face lit up. "They'll be won over like me."

"Mrs. Fox wouldn't want people just poking around," she said. "Although," she speculated, narrowing her eyes, "she did like you."

"And who wouldn't like lovable old me?" Steven questioned.

"Hah!" answered Leah.

" 'Hah' to you — see you after school," Steven said.

"I'm going over to Mrs. Fox's," she said.

He half turned, his square frame filling the doorway. "Are you keeping up with your schoolwork?"

"I'm doing okay." She concentrated on the last of her cereal, not wanting to tell him about her low score in math.

"Well, you know what Mom and Dad said," he warned. "If you bring home any more failing grades, you'll be grounded again."

"I know," she said miserably. "I'm trying."

"Good. You can do it." He winked and was out the door.

Easy for Mr. Top Grades to say, she thought glumly, as she set her bowl in the sink and filled it with water. Although she had to admit her English grades were much better, and she loved the animal unit they were studying in science. Maybe she could get good grades after all. Mrs. Fox had helped her a lot. Well, she thought, squaring her shoulders and heading out the door, if she could improve in English and science, she could improve in math. She'd better take Mr. Gonser's advice and enroll in the math tutoring program.

At school she kept strictly to herself. Even though Terry came up to talk to her she answered only in monosyllables. She was still too angry at all of them to be friendly. As usual school was boring, but without friends, it was worse than she'd ever imagined.

In science class Leah did manage to forget her troubles for a little while. Mr. Gonser had invited an interesting speaker, Ms. Hensley, who described ferrets and their habits and had brought along a cage containing one of the furry creatures. Ms. Hensley, a young woman who wore oversized glasses and a trim gray-striped suit, kept seventeen ferrets in her basement.

Leah studied the ferret as it lay curled up asleep in its cage, unaware of the class's stares. The ferret's long body and snout resembled a weasel, which it was related to.

"At present," Ms. Hensley said, "my ferrets sleep most of the day, but at dinnertime I let them out for about two hours. They tear through the house, racing from one room to another. Then I let them romp in a playhouse I had built for them with some hollow tubes to run through. After they've played, I feed them, and they're ready to sleep again." She chuckled, opening the cage and stroking the sleeping animal's head. "I have sort of a halfway house for ferrets. The other day a boy brought me two that his mother said he couldn't keep anymore, although I don't know why, since they make excellent pets."

After a few more facts Ms. Hensley asked if anyone had any questions. Leah was surprised at how much the kids wanted to know. She knew Mrs. Fox could have answered every question, too. Maybe she should tell Mr. Gonser about Mrs. Fox and he could invite her to speak. But she doubted if Mrs. Fox would accept. She was too private a person. How would she ever prove to people what a warm human being Mrs. Fox was?

Throughout the day her spirits sank even lower, but on the way home she straightened her shoulders. She had signs to post. Ozzie was still missing and Mrs. Fox was desperate to find him. Posting signs in the neighborhood was one thing she could do to help. And at least it would take her mind off her own loneliness.

15

Leah ran down Tall Trees Lane and into the house. She was sick of feeling sorry for herself. She needed to finish her Ozzie signs and she had received permission to post them on trees around the neighborhood. If Ozzie wasn't returned soon, it was likely he was gone for good.

Unbuttoning her heavy-knit sweater and draping it over a chair, she retrieved her posters from behind the door and placed them on the kitchen table. Using a ruler and her colored marking pens, she began to print the words:

LOST: LOVABLE COCKER SPANIEL

This black friendly puppy answers to the name "Ozzie" and is a special pet. If found, please call: 251–5382 or return to Mrs. Blanche Fox, 822 Tall Trees Lane.

Reward

Leah ended by putting a flourish on the word *reward*. She'd saved ten dollars from her baby-sitting money and she was sure Mrs. Fox would scrape together a small amount to give to Ozzie's finder.

She leaned back in her chair, holding up the poster and checking over the red-and-blue letter-ing. She hoped this notice would bring results. If only her friends knew the unhappiness they'd caused!

Leah poured herself a glass of milk and gazed out the window, studying the few crimson and gold leaves clinging to the maple's branches, but not really seeing the tree. Instead, she pictured her friends having a Coke at Sandy's and won-dered if they were having a good time without her. Her eyes shifted to the brown yard, the stubby grass, and the empty patio. Dad had stored the table and chairs for the winter. Winter, she thought gloomily. What an unhappy prospect! Even though she loved to cross-country ski and ice skate, it wouldn't be any fun alone.

School was lonely and hard, too. Math continued to trouble Leah, and she'd failed a quiz today. Her stomach churned, forming one big knot. She pushed aside the milk, unable to finish.

Leah shook her head to clear it. Now, she thought, there are problems to be tackled. She rose and gathered the posters. She must put them up before dark. If only someone would see the signs and return Ozzie. It wrenched her heart to see Mrs. Fox search every day, and every day come back empty-handed. Mrs. Fox had questioned people, too, but Ozzie had disappeared into thin air. Even the cats, Willie and Sima, seemed to miss the frisky little dog.

At the corner of Tall Trees Lane and Chestnut Road, Leah posted her first sign on a large oak. The large letters were sharp and clear and would surely catch the eye of someone who had seen Ozzie. Hurrying on to the next block, she put up a second poster.

The setting sun gave the gray-streaked sky a pink glow, and Leah buttoned up her sweater against the rising wind. On the next block holding a nail between her teeth, she positioned the sign on a tree trunk. But before she could remove her hammer from her back pocket, she glimpsed Rose-anne coming along the street. In the wind her blonde hair blew about her face and her plaid scarf sailed out behind her. Leah froze, rooted to the spot. Roseanne halted, too, clutching her books against her denim jacket.

For a moment the two girls stared at one another. But when a moving van rumbled past, the spell was broken. Leah removed the nail from between her teeth and began hammering up her sign. She lifted her chin, trying not to show how much she cared and how much she missed Roseanne. She wished Roseanne would just walk on. Grimly, she pounded in the nail, wondering if Roseanne had read the sign down the block about Ozzie. She hoped so. Then she might understand the heartbreak she'd caused Mrs. Fox.

Leah wanted to run away from Roseanne, but in her haste to finish, the posters that were under her arm slipped to the ground. She went on hammering, though, ignoring the fallen signs.

From the corner of her eye she noticed Roseanne standing as still as a statue. Was she silently laughing at her? What was she thinking? Why didn't she move on? Was Roseanne gloating like the day she'd seen Leah straining to lower the brass deer?

When the poster was secured to the tree, Leah stooped to pick up her signs. But when she reached out, she touched Roseanne's fingertips. Startled, she glanced up. Roseanne silently tucked a poster under her arm, and held out her hand for some tacks.

Leah's eyes grew wide. Quietly, she handed her the hammer and tacks.

"I'll fasten this sign on the tree in our front yard," Roseanne offered shyly. Her ivory face had a soft rose flush on her cheekbones, and her blue eyes searched Leah's face. "That is, if it's all right with you."

Leah nodded, unable to speak.

"I'll put up this sign, then help you with the others," Roseanne said softly.

"OK," Leah answered, smiling tremulously.

"Do you think Ozzie will turn up?" Roseanne's face wrinkled in a worried frown.

"These signs should help," Leah said, all at once not knowing what to say. Before, she'd always been able to chatter away like mad with Roseanne, but not now. Was it embarrassment? Or was it the cautious joy she felt? Was it possible Roseanne was really her friend again?

Roseanne took a step backward. "I'll nail these up, and . . . and . . ." Tears bordered her lashes. "Oh, Leah, I'm sorry that we hurt Mrs. Fox. We didn't know that the little dog wouldn't find his way back."

"I know," Leah said quietly. "I thought Ozzie would turn up, too."

"Leah," Roseanne cried, dropping her poster and dashing forward. "I want you to be my friend again."

Leah held out her arms and hugged Roseanne with all her might. "I've missed you, Roseanne."

"Let's never never let anything come between us again," Roseanne said firmly. She smiled through tears. "Not even Mrs. Fox."

"Not even Mrs. Fox," Leah murmured. She was so happy she thought her heart would burst.

16

On Monday after school, Leah hummed softly as she kneeled before the railing on Mrs. Fox's porch. Using white enamel, she painted one of the supports, and thought how wonderful the house was going to look. Gradually, carefully, she and Roseanne were becoming friends again. And even though her English grades never reached another A, still she was happier in school. She felt more sure of herself because she'd done a good job on the interview paper. It proved that she wasn't so dumb after all.

"You're quite a painter, Leah," Mrs. Fox said, coming out on the porch. "I should have given you my hat. You've got paint in your hair!" She folded her arms over her old sweater and gazed about. "My house has never looked so good." She nodded in appreciation, tucking a loose strand back into her thick braids. She clomped about in her heavy boots, admiring the work that had been done. "Yes, my house sparkles and I'm certain that I'm not the only one that's pleased." She chuckled. "The neighbors are probably ecstatic."

"Oh, yes," Leah agreed, laughing. "I saw Mrs. McBride peeking over the backyard fence, trying to find out what's going on over here." Her brush strokes moved faster, and she didn't dare look at Mrs. Fox. "Sometime," she said casually, "my mom and dad would like to come over and visit." Leah gave Mrs. Fox a side glance. "Would — would you mind?" she stammered.

"I'd like to meet your parents," Mrs. Fox replied softly.

Leah glanced up at her. "You would?" she asked eagerly.

"Yes, I would." Blanche Fox smiled. "I think it's about time I had some company. . . . Probably because I've enjoyed yours so much!"

Leah jumped up, waving her paint brush. "Why not have your other neighbors over, too? The cages are clean, the bushes trimmed, and," her eyes twinkled as she repeated Mrs. Fox's words, "the house is sparkling."

Mrs. Fox didn't reply. She pressed her lips together as she busily inspected the mailbox that Steven had straightened and painted.

"We could have a party," Leah said, trying to keep the excitement out of her voice, "and invite the people that live on this block. We could serve coffee and cake, and they could see your animals and meet you." Breathless, she stared at Mrs. Fox, willing her to say yes.

Blanche Fox snorted, sitting down on the first step and resting her elbows on her knees. "Do you think anyone would show up?"

"Oh, yes. Everyone," she said positively. "We could ask them to come Sunday afternoon."

"I don't know," Mrs. Fox answered doubtfully, reaching for Matilda who had sauntered out on the porch. She stroked the cat's gleaming gray coat, and her eyes darkened in thought. "Maybe — maybe," she hesitated, "we could give it a try."

Leah almost jumped up and down like a little kid. Now the neighbors would see what she saw, that Mrs. Fox was a wonderful person! Already she began to plan for Sunday. "What do you think we should serve?" she asked, her mind skittering ahead.

Mrs. Fox shrugged. "I used to entertain, but I haven't for years. Perhaps we should make it a simple drop-in on Sunday. We could have cake and coffee as you suggested."

"Yes, yes," Leah said, nodding vigorously. Suddenly she snapped her fingers. "An open house. I'll write the invitations and stick them in the neighbors' mailboxes."

Mrs. Fox sighed. "If you want to, Leah, but don't be disappointed if no one comes. I've kept to myself for so long that my neighbors know I didn't want anything to do with them. They're not likely to forget the past fifteen years in one afternoon." She gave Leah a knowing smile. "But you go ahead. I'll bake a cake, and at least we know that your parents will show up." Her small smile was wistful, as if she understood the ways of adults better than Leah.

Later, when Leah and Mrs. Fox sipped their tea, Mrs. Fox said, "I almost forgot to tell you, Leah. I got a call about Ozzie today. A little boy said he'd seen a spaniel pup on Elder Drive. I searched every inch of the block but didn't find him." She placed a work-worn hand over Leah's. "I never did thank you for putting up all the signs you made." Abruptly she rose. "I'm afraid Ozzie's lost for good." She rinsed her teacup beneath the faucet, then leaned heavily against the counter. "I miss the little fellow."

Leah stood up and put her arm around Mrs. Fox's shoulder.

Dry-eyed, Mrs. Fox glanced at her. "I'm fine, Leah."

"Don't give up," Leah said. "My friends are looking everywhere for Ozzie. They're sorry they untied Ozzie's rope."

"I know they are, and I'm glad you and Roseanne are friends again. I know how much you missed her." She gave Leah a quick smile. "Thanks for caring. And now," she said matter-of-factly, "to work! Would you help carry Jack's cage to the pickup truck? Our raccoon is ready for his home in the woods."

"He's well?" Leah asked in surprise. She'd grown so attached to all the animals that it was always hard to see one leave. "I'll miss Jack, but he'll be glad to be in the woods again."

"Yes, Jack is well," Mrs. Fox said drily. "I remember when I found him. He was thin and wouldn't eat. Now he has a ravenous appetite and paces the cage like a cat. He's ready for freedom."

Leah laughed. It was such a joy to see an animal get well. Even the blue jay that Mrs. McBride had brought over was screeching noisily and beginning to move his broken wing.

"I'll get my jacket," Leah said. In the hall she paused at Mr. McTavish's wire cage.

"Hello," the parrot squawked. "Hello."

"Hello," Leah replied. "This week I'm going to

teach you a new word, Mr. McTavish. Can you say 'welcome'?" She paused, enunciating more clearly. "Wel-come," she repeated.

Mr. McTavish cocked his emerald green head, and his beady eye glittered. "Hello," he said again. "Hello."

"Welcome. Welcome," Leah said. "We've got to get you ready for Sunday's open house!" She gazed at the brightly plumed parrot, but Mr. McTavish said nothing. Leah sighed. "We'll have another lesson tomorrow, Mr. McTavish." She scampered outside to help Mrs. Fox.

After setting the cage on the truck, Leah turned to leave. "I've got to get home, Mrs. Fox. I'd love to go out to the forest preserve with you, but I don't dare be late for supper. Nothing must go wrong this week. If I were grounded, what would we do about Sunday?"

Blanche Fox chuckled softly, jamming her old wide-brimmed hat over her braids. "I'll confess that my legs would shake if you weren't there, Leah."

"You'll be fine," Leah said reassuringly, but she knew she had to be by Mrs. Fox's side on Sunday. It would be a big day, and she wanted to be part of it.

Blanche Fox jumped into the truck. "See you tomorrow, Leah." She started the engine.

"Tomorrow," Leah called with a wave.

But as she hurried home, she thought about what Mrs. Fox had said. Maybe she was right. Maybe she had been a hermit too long. Maybe no one would come to the open house. How terrible that would be! Mrs. Fox would be crushed. And so would she.

17

During history class, as Leah put the finishing touches on the last invitation for Sunday's party, she half-listened to the Civil War song, "When Johnny Comes Marching Home." Miss Calvert was playing a scratchy tape about the Civil War, and she wasn't interested.

Leah swept a long strand of hair behind her ears and decided to add two last words to the invitation. *Please come.* She prayed that everything on Sunday would go all right. Let's see, she thought, she'd written in the address, date, and time. It all seemed correct as she scanned the invitation one last time:

MRS. BLANCHE FOX INVITES YOU TO AN
OPEN HOUSE
Sunday, November 9
822 Tall Trees Lane
2 to 5
Refreshments
It will be fun! Please come!

All at once Miss Calvert was alongside her desk, silently tapping Leah's paper. Guiltily Leah glanced at her and hastily tucked it away in her notebook. Miss Calvert raised her eyebrows, shook her head, and walked on. But somehow Leah didn't find her frown so forbidding anymore. Not since she'd been getting better grades.

During study hall, Leah was able to complete the invitations and address the envelopes. All she needed to do was to slip them in the neighbors' mailboxes.

In math class she was elated to have passed yesterday's quiz. Maybe the tutoring program was working.

When the last bell rang, she was so excited that she fairly flew out the door.

"Hey, Leah! Wait for me!" Roseanne called, catching up with her. "Where you going?"

"I need to deliver these invitations."

"Let's have a Coke first," Roseanne coaxed.

Leah shook her head. "After I finish, I promised Mrs. Fox I'd paint the backyard cages." She turned away.

"Leah, wait!"

"What?"

For a moment Roseanne was quiet, then she said softly, "I hope the open house is a smash."

Leah studied Roseanne's face. Suddenly Leah asked, "Roseanne, would you come?"

"Oh, could I?" she asked, her eyes big. "I mean, would it be all right?"

"Sure," Leah answered with a smile.

Roseanne hesitated. "How about Danielle?"

"What's past is past. I'd really like to see Danielle, too."

"Could the guys come also?"

"Sure." Leah smiled.

"You don't think Mrs. Fox would mind?"

"Not if you all come as friends."

Roseanne smiled, and shifted her books from one hip to the other. "Has Ozzie turned up?"

"No, not yet," Leah said. "She has had one or two calls because of the signs we posted," Leah added hopefully. But she was scared Ozzie was lost forever. Mrs. Fox didn't have many things to love in her life, and she needed him. He had a special place in her heart. Leah tried to reassure herself. "I think he'll come back."

"I hope you're right," Roseanne said wistfully. "I wish we'd never let him go."

Leah swallowed hard, not knowing what to say. She wished they hadn't, too. But the damage was done. She looked at Roseanne's stricken face.

"There's a big math test Monday, and even

though I've enrolled in the tutoring program I still don't understand the division of fractions. Would you help me?"

"I thought you'd never ask," Roseanne's face lit up. "I've offered to help you a million times."

"I know," Leah said resignedly. "I just wasn't ready."

Roseanne's smile widened. "I'll bring my book over Saturday afternoon and we'll go over fractions together. It's easy."

Easy for you, Leah thought glumly. Then she brightened. "We'll make fudge first," she said.

Roseanne wagged a finger beneath Leah's nose. "Fractions first, fudge later."

"OK, OK," Leah agreed, grinning. "I guess you're right. First the medicine, then the good stuff."

"See you tomorrow," Roseanne said, veering off in the opposite direction.

" 'Bye," said Leah. She felt good that Roseanne didn't resent Mrs. Fox anymore. She knew, too, that her friends felt bad about Ozzie. If only the pup would reappear, it would make a lot of people happy.

After the invitations had been delivered, she went to Mrs. Fox's, where she continued to paint, rake more leaves, and groom the animals. As she brushed the three cats, she thought that she must do this every day so they'd look their best on Sunday.

Taking Matilda on her lap, she combed the cat's short fur. Matilda looked so much better than when she'd first been found on the doorstep. Sadly, she thought how much she'd love to take Matilda, but as long as Mom was allergic to fur, she knew it was impossible. It was too bad. Everyone loved kittens, but old cats were hard to give away. Well, she thought, gently scratching behind Matilda's ears, when she was a vet, she'd own lots of dogs and cats.

The week whizzed by. Saturday morning, when she was helping Mrs. Fox move empty cages into the garage, a lean black man walked around the house. He wore a billed cap that matched his navy-blue uniform. "Hi," he said with a smile. "I think I've got someone in my van you'd like to see."

Mrs. Fox straightened, pushing back her wide-brimmed hat. "Who?" she asked gruffly.

"Come with me," he said lightly, turning and striding forward. Leah and Mrs. Fox gave each other a puzzled look but dutifully followed him. LONNIGAN'S TELEVISION REPAIR SERVICE was printed on the back of his uniform.

Standing on his hind legs looking out the van's window was Ozzie! Leah caught her breath, and

Mrs. Fox broke into a wide smile. She dashed forward, opened the door, and gathered Ozzie into her arms. The frantic dog licked her face, yipping joyfully.

"Ozzie! Ozzie!" Mrs. Fox exclaimed, holding her head back and laughing. "Where have you been?" Her eyes were bright as she looked questioningly at the serviceman.

"Came up to my house about a week ago, his fur all matted with burrs. I kept him in the garage and fed him, but he didn't eat much." He shook his head sympathetically at the memory. "Whimpered a lot, too. I could tell he missed his owner. I planned on taking him to the humane society tomorrow. Nice little fellow, but I've got a cat and don't need a dog, too."

Leah ran over to Ozzie and Mrs. Fox. Her fingers trembled as she rubbed his head and let him lick her cheek. "Ozzie! You rascal! Don't you know how much we missed you?"

In answer the spaniel yipped, his pink tongue wagging as he panted in excitement. Mrs. Fox set him on the ground. But Ozzie wouldn't remain still. He danced and yapped about her feet, almost jumping high enough to get back into her arms.

"I wouldn't have known who the pup belonged to," the repairman continued, "until I had a TV job over on Chestnut and saw the sign. Went right home and picked him up."

"Oh, thank you," breathed Leah. She turned to Mrs. Fox. "I'll go home and get my money."

"Oh, yes," Blanche Fox said gratefully, "we want to give you your reward."

"Forget it," the tall man said, slicing the air with his hand. "I don't want a single thing. I'm just tickled I found his real home." He laughed. "I can see he's in the right place now." With that he got into his van, touched his fingers to his visored cap, and backed out of the driveway.

Wreathed in smiles, Leah and Mrs. Fox went inside with Ozzie barking at their heels.

In the kitchen, while Mrs. Fox nuzzled Ozzie, Leah prepared a bowl of dog food and set down water for the thin pup. "We've got to fatten you up, Ozzie," she scolded gently.

Together she and Mrs. Fox watched Ozzie gobble his food. Leah leaned against the refrigerator and sighed with contentment. What a perfect end to a perfect day. If only the next day — and the open house — could go as well! A concerned frown creased her forehead. And why wouldn't things go all right, she asked herself silently, annoyed at her silly worrying. Yet a little voice inside her head nagged at her. How, she wondered fearfully, would the neighbors react to Mrs. Fox after they'd been ignored for fifteen years?

Late that afternoon Roseanne came over, and she and Leah worked for over an hour on the division of fractions.

At last Leah sank back in the kitchen chair, blowing a wisp of hair off her forehead. "I don't understand this dumb stuff." She gave a choked desperate laugh. For the first time in her life she really did want to do well. Instead, though, she said in an uncaring voice, "I'll just fail another test. No big deal. Let's quit and make fudge."

"Not until you've worked at least two more problems," Roseanne answered firmly. "We'll go through the steps together."

With a sigh, Leah gave a shrug of resignation and leaned forward. "OK, but only two more problems. I'm sick of fractions."

Concentrating, she followed Roseanne's explanation, then worked the second problem on her own. When her answer matched Roseanne's, she was delighted. She worked a third problem. Suddenly it was easy. With Roseanne's explanation and what she'd learned in the tutoring center, dividing fractions had finally become clear. What a dolt she'd been not to get help earlier!

"See?" Roseanne said. "You can do it if you want to, Leah."

"Now I know I'll do well on the test," Leah said, grinning.

"I know it, too," Roseanne responded. "I can see you understand. You'll do OK; I'll help you anytime that you want me to. We're best friends, aren't we?"

Leah nodded happily. "The best!" Her eyes met Roseanne's. Then she jumped up and set a bowl of walnuts before Roseanne. "Start cracking nuts for the fudge," she ordered.

Leah reached for the milk and poured it into a measuring cup. "Maybe," she admitted, "my counselor, my teachers, and my parents have been right all along. The tutoring has really been worth it." Standing at the stove, she stirred the fudge mix and milk until it came to a boil. "And with a little help from my friends I think I've got it made."

"I don't *think*," Roseanne agreed, her eyes twinkling. "I *know* you've got it made." She cracked a walnut, removed the pieces, and dropped them into a bowl.

Leah switched the topic to what was uppermost in her mind. "I hope the open house goes all right," she said in a small voice.

"Will you stop worrying?" Roseanne asked, popping nut meat into her mouth. "You'd think you were giving a party for the President! Just watch. The neighbors will all come out."

Unconvinced, Leah dumped the nuts into the rich chocolate and poured the fudge into a buttered pan. She wished she could be as sure as Roseanne about the neighbors.

18

Sunday afternoon, Leah dressed with care in a pale blue sweater and navy pleated skirt. She brushed her long chestnut brown hair, which swung softly over her shoulders, until the burnished copper highlights shone. She wondered if Terry would come to the open house. Terry. She smiled broadly. Why was she thinking about him? Hmmmf, she thought. Since when had she thought of Terry as anything but a friend? How ridiculous!

She grabbed her bag and ran out of the house. Steve, Mom, and Dad had promised to come over at three o'clock. At least she could count on them to meet Mrs. Fox, eat a piece of cake, and drink a cup of coffee.

When she got to Mrs. Fox's, she paused at Mr. McTavish's cage. "Wel-come," she said loudly. "Say it, Mr. McTavish. 'Welcome.'"

The parrot bent his head. "Hello," he said.

"Why are you so stubborn, Mr. McTavish? Say 'welcome.' "

But the parrot was silent, not uttering another word.

Going inside, Leah glanced about at the sparkling clean house.

In the dining room, the table gleamed with silver and china, and a fall bouquet was the centerpiece. Napkins were neatly fanned out at the end.

"Mrs. Fox," she sang out. "I'm here."

"Leah, I'm glad you're early," Blanche Fox said, hurrying out from the bedroom.

Leah's mouth dropped open. Never had she seen Mrs. Fox like this — she was dressed in a beautiful silk navy dress, navy heels, and navy hose.

Mrs. Fox gave her an amused look. "What are you staring at, girl?"

"Y-you," Leah stammered. "I've never seen you dressed up."

Mrs. Fox twirled about, her flared dress swirling. "Like it?"

"I-I love it," Leah said in astonishment, unable to believe the transformation. Mrs. Fox had on pale pink blush and lipstick, and a pair of pearl earrings. She'd even styled her hair. The usual heavy braids were loosely coiled, and soft waves framed her small face.

"Would you stop staring," Mrs. Fox asked with a glint of humor, "and set out the rest of the cups?"

Leah stirred herself. "Sure, sure," she said hastily, going to the breakfront.

This was going to be a lovely party, Leah thought, carefully removing the fragile cups. Better than she'd dared hope. It was almost time for the first guests, so she'd better hurry. The blue china on the white tablecloth looked delicate and almost transparent.

At two o'clock Leah glanced anxiously out the window. No one yet. Smiling, she joined Mrs. Fox in the living room to wait for the first caller. The rich aroma of coffee filled the house. Everything was ready. She couldn't wait!

By two-fifteen, she squirmed uneasily in her chair. Someone should have arrived by now.

By two-thirty, however, her heart began to pound and her hands became sweaty. Where was everyone? Where was *someone?* She stole a despairing glance at Mrs. Fox. What must she be thinking? Mrs. Fox, however, quietly turned a page of her book, apparently unconcerned.

Leah felt her throat tighten. After all their hard work, their neighbors weren't coming. Disappointed, she tried to swallow away the lump in her throat. Her worst nightmare was coming true!

"Welcome!" Mr. McTavish screeched, breaking the silence. Leah held her breath. Did she hear footsteps?

The doorbell chimed. Yes, she thought in exultation. At last someone was coming!

Mrs. Fox stood up, glancing at Leah. She grinned and went to the door. Leah trailed behind.

In stepped Mrs. McBride, her big frame blocking the stream of light from the doorway. "I can't stay," she announced abruptly. "Just brought you these!" She thrust a fistful of coupons into Mrs. Fox's hand. "You can save money on dog and cat food. Thought you could use them." She peered around at the living room and dining room. "Since you were so nice to the blue jay I thought it was the least I could do."

"Let me pour you a cup of coffee," Mrs. Fox urged. "You don't need to rush away. Let me show you how well Mr. Grinch is doing."

"Mr. Grinch?" she asked, her mottled face screwing up in suspicion. "Who's Mr. Grinch?"

"That's the blue jay. He's a grinch — always complaining. His wing has healed nicely, and he'll soon be able to fly free." She led Mrs. McBride out back.

"Welcome!" Mr. McTavish squawked again. Leah smiled, pleased that he'd said the new word at just the right time. Again the doorbell rang.

She opened the door to Roseanne and her parents, and while pouring them coffee, Mr. McTavish's "welcome" echoed throughout the house again. She smiled at Roseanne, thrust a Coke into her hand, and ran to answer the door.

Soon the house and yard were filled with neighbors. They laughed and chatted, peered into the cages, and talked to the animals. Leah was surprised at the number of neighbors who had responded to the invitations. And to think she'd been worried. True, some neighbors were wary and not too friendly, but they were too curious to stay away.

Her mom and dad and Steven entered by the back door. "Hi, Sis," Steven said exuberantly. "I was showing Mom and Dad what I'd done to fix this place up."

"We did a lot of painting, didn't we?" Leah added.

Mrs. Dvorak's eyes twinkled. "I'm proud of both of you. I'm glad you helped Mrs. Fox. I had no idea how hard she works to maintain such a large menagerie."

"I fixed the porch railing, too," Steven interrupted proudly.

"I can see that," Mr. Dvorak said, ruffling up his son's hair.

"Hmmm, what kind of cake? Chocolate?" a man standing behind Leah asked.

"Chocolate fudge," Leah said, slicing a piece and turning to offer it to him. "Oh, hi, Mr. Volini," she said, brightening when she recognized the policeman from down the block. Officer Volini was a nice man, she thought, remembering that once he'd rescued a cat from a tree.

"Leah Dvorak?" he asked, raising bushy brows over his dark warm eyes. "You've grown up! You're quite the young lady!"

She smiled. She was glad he'd come.

"Is there any more coffee?" Mrs. O'Bannion asked, holding out an empty cup.

"I'll get more." Leah smiled at Terry's mother. "Excuse me," she said to Mr. Volini, picking up the silver coffeepot and quickly threading her way through the people who now crowded around the dining room table.

In the kitchen she refilled the silver pot, and when she returned Danielle, Mike, and Terry had just come in from outdoors. Even though it was November, the sunny day was quite warm, and there were as many neighbors outside as in. She could barely keep track of everyone.

"I'm ready for a second piece of cake," Danielle said, pushing her way forward. Roseanne joined them, too, and Leah felt a warm glow in having her friends all around her.

"I told you the open house would be a smash," Roseanne said, squeezing Leah around the waist.

"You look nice, Leah," Danielle said, then leaned over, whispering in Leah's ear. "Is that really the 'Witch of Tall Trees Lane'?" she asked, staring wide-eyed at Mrs. Fox, who was talking to Mrs. McBride. "I thought she was old."

"I kept trying to tell you that Mrs. Fox wasn't old," Leah said in mock severity, trying not to smile. "But you guys wouldn't listen." She noticed Mrs. Fox leading Mrs. McBride over to Matilda, where the gray cat reclined in the corner rocker.

"You know, Mrs. Fox isn't bad," Terry said. "After today I guess she won't be called a witch again!"

Leah felt her heart swell with pride for Mrs. Fox. She was glad her friends could see how kind and warm she was — and how wonderful her animals were, too.

"She's got a cute dog," Roseanne went on. "I'm so glad Ozzie was found."

"Did you see all the animals she takes care of?" Terry asked in an eager voice. "I had a long chat with Frank, the woodchuck, and I think he understood every word I said."

Mrs. McBride's face beamed as she bustled past Leah, cradling Matilda in her arms. "Mrs. Fox said I could adopt her," she crowed. Heads turned. "Isn't she a beauty?" she asked the entire room. The cat raised her head, then nestled back into the soft niche of Mrs. McBride's arms.

"Here," Mrs. Fox said with a laugh. "I'm returning these cat food coupons. You'll need them to stock up for Matilda. She's got a hefty appetite."

Mrs. McBride stuffed them into her pocket. "Got to go, folks, and show my baby her new home." She smiled briefly at Mrs. Fox. "I hadn't planned to stay this long, and I certainly hadn't planned to go home with a cat!"

"Come back anytime," Mrs. Fox said warmly.

After Mrs. McBride had sailed out with Matilda, Ozzie scampered in and sat at Mr. Volini's feet. He laughed when Ozzie sat up, begging with his front paws. "That's a cute pooch, you've got," he said. "I own two dogs and a cat myself. Believe me, when I saw the sign for your lost puppy, I was plenty worried." He paused, looking at Mrs. Fox. "I searched the East Woods but didn't turn up anything." He held out his cup to Leah for more coffee but kept his eyes fastened on Mrs. Fox. "By the way, is there anything I can do to help out with your animals? I'm a pretty good carpenter."

"I can manage," Mrs. Fox said, "but thanks."

"You sure now?" Mr. Volini asked.

Mrs. Fox smiled and took a sip of coffee. Then she said, "I'd hate to lose Ozzie again. He hates the rope, but really . . ." She hesitated, then said, "No, I can't think of any work around here."

"How about a dog run?" he said eagerly. "I'd be happy to build you one."

"You would?" Blanche Fox asked. "That would be wonderful, but I can't ask you to do such a big job."

"But I like building things," he insisted. "I want to."

"We-e-ll," she said slowly, "if you're sure you don't mind." She reached down and petted Ozzie. "Ozzie would love it."

Pete Volini chuckled. "If you save me a piece of cake I'll be over tomorrow. It's my day off."

"You've got a deal."

"We need to be going, Mrs. Fox. Thanks for the lovely afternoon," Madeline Dvorak said, standing with her husband's arm around her. "Perhaps you could come over to our house sometime — maybe for some kolaches?" She smiled at Leah. "My daughter has kept you to herself far too long."

For a moment a shadow flitted across Blanche Fox's face. "No," she said thoughtfully, "it's my fault. I've kept to myself too long. I'd love to, Mrs. Dvorak."

" 'Bye, Mrs. Fox," Steven said. "Don't give your deer anything more to eat." He grinned, halting halfway out the door. "People have been feeding Flora all afternoon."

"I won't give Flora another bite," Blanche Fox said, holding up her hand. "Thanks for everything, Steven!"

After the last guest had left, Leah helped Mrs. Fox clean up. "The neighbors like you," she said, a lilt in her voice.

"Some of them really do," she answered in wonder. "Thanks to you, Leah. This was your idea. Alone, I'd never have had the nerve to break the ice." Mrs. Fox gently laid her hand over Leah's. "You're my lovely little friend, Leah. You'll always have a special place in my heart. Today has been marvelous." She stopped. Ozzie settled at her feet, whimpering for his supper. "And you and I will always be friends. Nothing can change that."

"Nothing?" asked Leah.

"I promise," said Mrs. Fox. She put her arm around Leah's shoulders and hugged her. For a long moment they were quiet. Then Mrs. Fox gently pushed her away. "All right!" She cleared her throat. "Let's clean up this mess!"

APPLE®PAPERBACKS

Pick an Apple and Polish Off Some Great Reading!